ELVIS
*and the
Tropical
Double Trouble

**Center Point
Large Print**

Also by Peggy Webb
and available from Center Point Large Print:

Elvis and the Dearly Departed
Elvis and the Grateful Dead
Elvis and the Memphis Mambo Murders

ELVIS
*and the
Tropical
Double Trouble

Peggy Webb

CENTER POINT LARGE PRINT
THORNDIKE, MAINE

This Center Point Large Print edition
is published in the year 2012 by arrangement with
Kensington Publishing Corp.

Copyright © 2011 by Peggy Webb.

The text of this Large Print edition is unabridged.
In other aspects, this book may vary
from the original edition.
Printed in the United States of America
on permanent paper.
Set in 16-point Times New Roman type.

ISBN: 978-1-61173-291-7

Library of Congress Cataloging-in-Publication Data

Webb, Peggy.
Elvis and the tropical double trouble / Peggy Webb. — Center Point large print ed.
p. cm.
ISBN 978-1-61173-291-7 (library binding : alk. paper)
1. Beauty operators—Fiction. 2. Cousins—Fiction. 3. Basset hound—Fiction.
   4. Murder—Investigation—Fiction. 5. Tupelo (Miss.)—Fiction. 6. Large type books.
   I. Title.
PS3573.E1985E5857 2011
813′.54—dc23

2011035832

Elvis' Opinion #1 on the Valentines, Manicures, and Mooreville's Royalty

Ever since I used my famous nose to crack the Memphis Mambo Murder Case, things have gone to the dogs around here. And I don't mean to a musical genius in a basset hound suit, either. (That would be yours truly.)

To hear my human mom (that would be Callie Valentine Jones, owner of the best little beauty shop this side of the Mason-Dixon Line) tell it, life just couldn't get any better. She thinks she's happy since she said "The Last Farewell" to Jack (my human daddy) up in Memphis, but I know better. When she's not giving New York hairdos to Mooreville's finest and doling out the dough for her mama's little gambling escapades—and every other kind of escapade Ruby Nell Valentine can think of—she's sitting on the front porch swing with a faraway look in her eyes that says, "Stuck on You."

Listen, I know she believes Jack is finally going to give her a divorce so she can have her heart's desire with somebody who won't spend more time in the world's underbelly avoiding bullets than he does in the gazebo with Callie and her "Ain't nothin' but a hound dog" best friend. (I'm not even going to talk about Hoyt, that ridiculous cocker spaniel pretender to my throne, and the seven silly cats who took up residence with us when Callie rescued them and dragged them home.)

Believe me, Jack's face said it all when Callie and the rest of our gang headed home from Memphis—"There Goes My Everything." A man that smitten is not going to let his woman go, no matter how noble he thinks the gesture might be.

I'm trying to teach Jack and Callie to be thankful for what they've got—each other plus a suave, famous Rock 'n' Roll King who is content to live a dog's life in order to make his humans happy. Instead, they're intent on turning everything upside down to get what they think Callie wants. A child. Someone just like the short, not-too-bright little person who makes car noises all day long, smears peanut butter on my pink satin guitar-shaped pillow, pulls my mismatched ears, runs Tonka trucks up the legs of Callie's customers, and generally has turned everything upside down here at Hair.Net.

This particular little person is David. He was part of the package when his mom, Darlene (Callie's new manicurist), moved in lock, stock, and uppity Lhasa apso.

That would be William, who claims he's the Dalai Lama reincarnate. He's prancing around here, even as I speak, acting like he outranks the King. I thought he'd get the message when I howled "The Great Pretender," but he just did his

6

silly Lhasa flop that made Callie say, "Isn't he the cutest little dog?"

Cute, my slightly crooked hind leg. "Don't step on my blue suede shoes" is what she ought to be saying. That silly fuzzball's motto is "Rip It Up."

Mine is "Suspicious Minds." Listen, you can't trust a dog with a bushy tail. What's the use of a tail that can't point to rabbits? Or thump the floor like a drum? Or whack your human mom's legs to let her know you love her?

Wait till Callie finds out William sneaked into the beauty shop closet and chewed the toe out of her favorite Steve Madden moccasins. She loves her designer shoes.

But even with that dumb dog chewing up everything in sight and trying to steal my spotlight, and with David trying to pull my tail, I have to admit business has picked up around Hair.Net. Ever since Fayrene's daughter moved back home with her entourage (which includes a cat named Mal, which I'm not even going to dignify with a comment) and started dispensing Atlanta nail art, we've been booked to the hilt. Everybody who is anybody comes here to have Darlene paint witches and pumpkins on their toes. And while they're at it, they end up getting a new hairdo for Halloween.

Business is popping over at Gas, Grits, and Guts, too. People have been coming from Mantachie and Saltillo and even as far off as Red

Bay, Alabama, to admire Fayrene and Jarvetis' disco ball dance trophy. They hung it over the pickled pigs' lips, then proceeded to spotlight it so it would send rainbows over the Vlasic pickles and Lay's potato chips. My best friend, Trey (Jarvetis' redbone hound), tells me that Fayrene and Jarvetis (Mooreville's answer to royalty) are acting like lovebirds these days in spite of the fact that work is progressing on the séance room he said she'd build onto the back of their convenience store over his dead body.

And speaking of dead bodies . . . ever since Charlie Valentine thought Ruby Nell was going to join the body count during the Memphis Mambo Murders, he's back to being her best friend as well as the backbone of the entire Valentine family. As a matter of fact, he's planning to take her to the undertakers' convention in the Yucatan.

That leaves only one Valentine unaccounted for—Lovie, Callie's 190-pound, over-the-top flamboyant cousin. Currently she's in the Yucatan at Rocky's archeological dig promoting an agenda that features the love of her life discovering her "national treasure." She had that tattooed on her bombshell hips when we left off trying to catch a killer long enough to have a little fun up on Beale Street in Memphis. Personally, I think the "national treasure" ought to be added to the list of world wonders.

Here comes that five-year-old, pretending he's a Peterbilt rig. I'd escape through the doggie door and mosey on down to see what's cooking with my cute Frenchie (that would be Ann-Margret) and my five handsome progeny, but somebody has to keep things straight around here. Ruby Nell will be here any minute. She called to say she wanted to get spiffied up for her trip, but you can bet she's up to something. And I'm just the dog to find out. These mismatched radar ears miss nothing.

Well, bless'a my soul. The little person is carrying a cone of vanilla ice cream. That goofy Lhasa just waves his useless, ostentatious tail, but I know opportunity when it knocks.

I heft myself off my cushion, hum a few bars of "(Let Me Be Your) Teddy Bear," then mosey on over to see if the short person will let me lick ice cream off his elbows.

Chapter 1

Mooreville Gossip, Mexican Capers, and Misbehaving Mamas

Mooreville was edging toward fame with the disco ball dance trophy at Gas, Grits, and Guts, plus my dog Elvis, who thinks he's the King of Rock 'n' Roll. But I put it on the map when I hired an Atlanta manicurist who paints roses with faux jewels—and everything else you can imagine—on my customers' nails. My little beauty shop is now the talk of northeast Mississippi.

When I hired Darlene Johnson Lawford Grant to enhance the beauty experience of my clients at Hair.Net, I never figured on getting another menagerie plus a cherub/holy terror on chubby, dimpled legs. (Her son, David, from what Darlene terms her "second and final" marriage.)

Not that I'm complaining. In fact, just the opposite. Having a five-year-old running around the shop is almost like having my own little boy. Now that Jack Jones has promised a divorce and Luke Champion is acting like he's my personal prize stallion (he's a vet, which explains the animal analogy), I see my most cherished goal—motherhood—just over the horizon.

The only hitch is that I keep seeing my aspiring stallion-in-hot-pursuit as a delicious-looking blonde confection you admire through the window, but never get the burning desire to reach in and take a bite of.

On the other hand, just let my almost-ex come within spitting distance, and I want to eat him up, starting with his dark, always mussed hair and ending with his size twelve feet, which just about says it all.

But where Jack's concerned, I've decided to make *no* my new middle name. After all, everybody in the know in Mooreville's society considers me an entrepreneur on the upswing since Hair.Net got a manicurist. I'd be featured in the newspaper if Mooreville had one. Which is not likely in the next fifty years, considering Darlene and David are the biggest population explosion we've had in ten years. And they only brought the live body count up to six hundred fifty-two.

Holy cow, listen to me, thinking in body counts. I'm turning over a new leaf. Now that we've put the Peabody murderer behind bars, I'm giving up crime. Period. Unless you consider it criminal to amass the stash of cash I'm saving so I can hit the after-Thanksgiving shoe sales next month.

The sight of Mama in her red Mustang distracts me from thoughts of cute designer shoes. She's driving with the top down. Anybody else her age would drive with the top up. Shoot, they wouldn't even have a convertible in the first place. But that's Mama, sassy all over, and I have to say I'm glad. In this day and age, a little joie de vivre can take you a long way past the blues.

Mama's wearing a flaming red caftan, which matches her car, but clashes with her hair. I might tell her, depending on what kind of mood she's in. She doesn't always take criticism well, even if it's well meant. Which mine most certainly is. My motto is *Be nice to everybody.*

There's too little kindness in this world, and I try to do my part to spread it around.

Mama bursts through the front door and charges in like she owns the place. "I want the works."

"Mama, whatever happened to *hello?*"

"Flitter, everybody here knows who I am." Mama sashays over to the manicure table to see what color Darlene is painting Fayrene's fingernails. "Is that green?"

Well, naturally. Fayrene always decks herself out in the color of money.

"It's called peacock." Fayrene holds up her left hand. "It matches the new swimsuit cover-up I bought for my trip to the undertakers' convention."

For once Mama is speechless. If I recall, she never invited Fayrene, even if they are best friends.

"You didn't think I'd let you go to Cozumel without me, did you, Ruby Nell?" Fayrene blows on her left hand, though she knows good and well I've installed the latest technology, a nail dryer in pink, which happens to be my signature color, as well as Elvis' (my dog *and* the real King). Plus, it matches my loveseats with the hot pink vinyl covers.

"Besides," Fayrene adds, "that hammering over at Gas, Grits, and Guts is driving me crazy. As much as I want a séance room, I need some rest and respiration."

Relaxation, I hope, but you never can tell.

Maybe Fayrene's having breathing problems I don't know about. Which is highly unlikely. The grapevine in Mooreville is alive and well. Not that I gossip. Far from it. But I pride myself on having created a spa-like atmosphere in Hair.Net. (That's why I painted a beach scene on one wall.) I want my customers to be totally relaxed and to feel free to tell me everything.

"Mother's horoscope said she'd be traveling to hot climes this month." Darlene consults the stars daily. I didn't know this when I hired her, but I was tickled pink to find it out. Any woman in touch with the stars is a welcome addition to Hair.Net.

Besides, Darlene's a natural blonde with flawless skin and thick hair cut in long layers, perfect for her pretty little heart-shaped face. With her angelic looks and unflappable personality, she's drawing customers in here like there's no tomorrow. Even the men are abandoning the Mooreville Barber Shop to come here for a great cut from yours truly and a good gander at Darlene in her slim-cut jeans and Texas style, genuine alligator-skin boots. She and Lovie have a lot in common.

The last two days, though, Darlene's been looking a bit frazzled. I can't help but notice how relieved she looks that her mother is talking about leaving the country.

Currently Darlene, her son, and their

menagerie are living with Fayrene and Jarvetis. I guess they're feeling a little crowded over there. That will happen after about a week of company. And I know for a fact she's already been with her parents for three weeks.

My next project is to help Darlene find a little house with rent she can afford.

Darlene's unfazed when Mama plucks some Persian pink polish right out from under her nose, then proceeds to open the bottle and paint her own nails.

"Mama, if you'll care to remember, Darlene's the manicurist. Besides, that color clashes with your caftan."

"Since when is it a crime to try out a nail color in my own daughter's beauty shop? And for your information, if I want beauty advice, I'll ask for it."

As if that didn't announce her mood loud and clear, Mama flounces into my chair, snatches up a hand mirror, and views the back of her head like it's the burning of Chicago and I've personally lit the torch.

"I can't do a thing with my hair. You made a miswhack the last time."

"That's not even a word, Mama. And even if it was, I never miswhack."

I cinch the haircutting apron around her neck a little tighter than usual. Listen, I may be a pushover when it comes to Jack and babies and

Elvis and stray cats and dogs—well, to just about everything—but I have my limits. And being called anything less than a total expert with hair is one of them.

I'm so good, my older customers make post mortem hair appointments while they're still alive. I have a whole shelf devoted to the special color blends I use on some of my customers (Bitsy Morgan and Mabel Moffett, to name two) in case I'm out of current stock if they die unexpectedly and need a little touch-up.

If you're wondering, I also fix up hair and makeup of the deceased over in Tupelo at Uncle Charlie's Eternal Rest Funeral Home.

"What do you want me to do today, Mama?"

"Take an inch off, color me jet black, and loan me about five hundred."

There goes my after-Thanksgiving shoe shopping spree.

"Holy cow, you'll only be gone a few days."

"It's for incidentals."

"How many incidentals can you buy, Mama?"

"You never know. I hear Cozumel is a shopper's paradise. I might need six hundred."

At this rate, I'm going to have to go to the Yucatan to keep up with my money.

Besides, Mama's not going to like her hair black. Knowing her, she'll get a thousand miles away, then call me to fly down and turn her into a redhead.

"Black's too harsh for your face, Mama."

"It's my hair. Besides, while I'm south of the border, I want to look like a señorita."

"There's no use arguing with Ruby Nell." Fayrene prances over, plops herself into the empty chair next to Mama, then proceeds to hold her hands out to admire her green nails. "Every time I argue with her, it just irrigates the tar out of her."

Nobody raises an eyebrow. Around here, we're used to Fayrene's rearrangement of the English language.

"Still, it's my job as a hair professional to steer my customers to a flattering color."

"Carolina, I'm not a paying customer." Mama always calls me by my real name when she's mad, though I can't think of a thing I've done to get on her bad side except continue divorce proceedings with Jack Jones. She thinks he walks on water. "I don't know if I want to go jet black or raven."

The phone rings and I'm relieved to abandon my losing battle over Mama's disastrous hair choice. Lovie's name pops up on the caller ID.

"Callie, is the speaker on?"

"You don't have to shout, Lovie. I can hear you. And, no, the speaker's not on."

"Turn it on. I want everybody in Mooreville to know what's going on down here."

"Don't you even want to know who's in the shop?"

"I don't care. I need some love advice. The more the better."

"Hang on."

I might as well turn the speaker on. Mama's leaning over so far trying to eavesdrop, she's about to fall out of her chair. Plus Fayrene and Darlene are all ears.

I'm glad I don't feel the need to spread around my love life, or the lack thereof since Jack walked out. But my cousin enjoys being a one-woman show. She says it's good for business (she's the best caterer in the South), but personally I think she's just trying to cover up that big soft heart of hers, which makes her open her arms—and other body parts I'm too much of a lady to mention—to anybody who needs a dose of "Love Me Tender."

That's one reason I'm pulling so hard for Rocky Malone. He's the first man who has ever treated my cousin like the treasure she is. Besides, he's the kind of gentleman who would take good care of a woman. Plus, he's a very fine archeologist with a good shot at becoming world-renowned if things go well at his Mayan dig.

I put the phone on speaker. "You can broadcast to the masses now, Lovie."

"We've got everything down here—romantic sunsets over the water, a lovers' moon over the Mayan ruins, privacy out the wazoo—and

Rocky's not even close to discovering the national treasure."

"I thought he was searching for a lost city," Fayrene says.

"It's the lost tomb of the Nine Lords of the Night," Lovie tells her.

Mama chimes in. "The national treasure is my niece's *you know what,* Fayrene. She had it tattooed."

"Where?" Darlene wants to know.

"In Memphis," I tell her, but Lovie says, "On my hips, one word on each. About as close to the Holy Grail as you can get."

"The Holy Grail?" Fayrene looks puzzled, and her daughter says, "Mother, don't ask. I'll tell you later."

"I've tried everything," Lovie says. "When I went skinny dipping, Rocky ran to get me a bathrobe. And the only rise my Dance of the Seven Veils got out of him was to get up and turn down the lights in case somebody was looking in the window."

"I think that's sweet, Lovie," I tell her. "Rocky's an old-fashioned gentleman." Something my almost-ex never was.

Lovie says a word that should not be broadcast over the speakerphone.

Here I am doing everything I can to reassure her, when Fayrene pops up with, "Got any cards? I used to play strip poker with Jarvetis."

I don't even want to picture that.

I'm thinking this whole speakerphone conversation was a bad idea, when little David wanders into the room trailing Elvis. Could it get any worse? Now I'm a party to polluting the mind of the innocent, plus my dog has ice cream all over his muzzle. Thank goodness, Darlene jerks up her son and whisks him to the back room.

"Flitter, Fayrene," Mama says. "Anybody can play strip poker. Try a little lap dance, Lovie."

I don't even pretend her suggestion shocks me. Ever since I saw Mama doing the mambo up in Memphis with Mr. Whitenton, nothing shocks me where she's concerned. Though I'm happy to report that after she found out Thomas Whitenton was not the gentleman we first thought, she hasn't invited him back to her farm. Or any other place that I know of. Unless she's keeping secrets. Which she's perfectly capable of doing.

"Aunt Ruby Nell, when are you and Daddy flying down?"

"Day after tomorrow, Lovie. Charlie wants to have plenty of time to tour Rocky's dig at Tulum before the undertakers' convention."

"That's great. Callie, why don't you come?"

I'm just getting ready to say *I can't leave Hair.Net* when Mama says, "Fayrene's coming, too. By the time we get there, we'll have a seduction strategy."

Holy cow! This trip has disaster written all over it. When it comes to a choice between taking care of business in Mooreville and preventing Lovie from implementing Mama's seduction strategy in the Yucatan, there's no contest.

"I'll be there, Lovie."

My dog prances by, looking miffed. I swear, he acts like he thinks I ought to buy him a ticket, too. Which is perfectly ridiculous.

On the other hand, Tulum is filled with the bones of antiquity. And Elvis loves old bones.

Chapter 2

Suitcases, Studs, and Traveling Dogs

Mama is the last customer to leave the shop. She exits with raven hair—which I have to say looks good on her, thanks to yours truly—and more than half my shoe budget. The minute she jumps into her convertible for the short drive to her farm, I set about preparing for my departure to tropical climes.

Leaving home for a few days is not as easy as it sounds. First, I have to reschedule my hair appointments. Next, I explain to Darlene that my customers like to congregate at Hair.Net, whether they have an appointment or not.

"They love to just lounge around on my pink

vinyl loveseats and discuss the latest doings in Mooreville."

"In other words, gossip."

I can tell by Darlene's face and tone of voice she's not being mean. If she was, I just wouldn't leave her in charge. Period.

"Around here we consider it selfish not to share the news." I motion Darlene to follow me into the break room where I open the refrigerator door and point out a big pitcher of punch. "This is Lovie's Prohibition Punch. The recipe is tacked to the wall by the sink. Make sure the pitcher is filled at all times. My customers like to refresh themselves when they come here."

Darlene leans over the pitcher and takes a whiff. "In other words, drink."

I'm beginning to think she has a droll sense of humor.

"Let's just say they like to get happy. While I'm gone, continue to be your cheerful self and make everybody welcome."

"I can do that with one hand tied behind my back."

Darlene's a chip off her mama's block. Next to Mama, Fayrene is the bossiest, most take-charge woman I know.

Still, I've never left Hair.Net in anybody else's hands. I've always just shut down the shop when I'm leaving town.

The thought of not being here to personally handle every little thing makes me want to pour myself a big glass of Prohibition Punch. Plus, between Mama's loan and Lovie's crusade to discover and rev up Rocky's libido, this has turned out to be a stressful day. I'm reaching for two glasses, one for me, one for Darlene, when my cell phone rings.

It's Jack.

"Callie, I'm coming by to see you." Since when has my almost-ex ever issued a warning? This must be serious. "Are you at the shop?"

I can picture it now. Jack roaring up on his Harley making me go limp in front of my newly hired manicurist.

"I'm just leaving," I tell him.

"I'll see you at the house, then."

Thank goodness, he no longer has a key. I've had the locks changed. Still, a little thing like that never stopped Jack Jones.

Darlene leaves with David and William while I make sure everything is shipshape at the shop. Satisfied, I snap on Elvis' leash, and then lock up and head home. Which just happens to be only three minutes away.

My house is the most charming in all of Lee County; I don't care if I do say so myself. It's a white clapboard cottage with wraparound front porch. My inviting front porch alone makes the house worth its price—old brick floors, rocking chairs, chrysanthemums in fall colors blooming in pots all over the place. And, best of all, a porch swing screams *sit a spell, relax.*

Who should be sitting there but Jack Jones. Elvis runs over for a huge portion of petting, then races into the back yard to terrorize the cats and poor, gullible Hoyt, my cocker spaniel rescue. Jack just sits there watching me.

If I told you what the swing was screaming now, I'd be blushing down to the tips of my red Jimmy Choo stilettos.

"Do those rosy cheeks mean you're glad to see me?"

Well, shoot. It looks like I've got a long way to go before I can make *no* my middle name.

"For your information, my flush has nothing to do with you. If you'll care to remember, Friday is my big day at Hair.Net. I've been working hard. That's all."

Jack moves—swift, silent, and deadly as his code name (Black Panther, which I only found out a few weeks ago in Memphis). One minute he's on the swing, the next he's standing so close you couldn't get a straw between us.

"I wish you'd quit looking at me like that."

His grin is positively wicked. "Like what?"

"You know." I back toward the front door. "Since you're here, you might as well come in and have something cool to drink."

He follows me inside where I discover my

lemonade half gone and a glass on the table that I know good and well I didn't leave there. I'm a neat person, and never leave my house with the china out of place.

I'm not even going to ask how he got in. Instead, I pour myself a glass without even offering one to him.

I wish I could act cool and collected, but I reckon I'm the kind of woman who lets every little emotion show. Currently, my chief one is a Titanic-size ambivalence.

While I gulp down my drink, Jack stands in the doorway and watches my throat work. Finally, I finish my drink and hold the cool, damp glass against my hot cheek.

He stalks over, takes the glass, then puts his hand over the damp spot I've left on my cheek.

"Cal . . ." I wish he wouldn't call me that. It makes me want to light candles, then climb into a big bubble bath. With him. "I know I promised to sign the divorce papers . . ."

"Don't you dare tell me you've changed your mind."

"Are you that anxious to hook up with Luke Champion?"

"What I do or do not do with Champ is none of your business."

"*Do not do?* That's an interesting choice of words."

I don't know whether to show him the door or

show him the bed. That's how crazy Jack Jones makes me.

"For your information, Champ wants to give me an engagement ring."

"And you've said no."

"I didn't say that."

"You also didn't say, 'he's giving me a ring' or 'I'm getting engaged.'"

I turn my back to him, march over to the sink, and start washing the glasses. Two is so much cozier than one. Two glasses on the table, two toothbrushes in the bathroom, two heads on the pillow.

Jack comes up behind me, and I just stand there with my hands wrapped around his glass, hoping he doesn't touch me.

"Cal. I didn't come to fight." Thank goodness, he's not touching.

"Why did you come?"

"To tell you I'm leaving tonight. Company business."

There's no need to ask where. He won't tell. The Company won't let him tell. I guess not knowing is a good thing. When we were still living under the same roof, I used to lie awake at night wondering where he was and what he was doing.

Now that I've found out he works undercover, is considered one of The Company's most lethal operatives, and nobody who knows the particulars of what he's doing is safe, I still lie awake at night. But now, I'm no longer wondering where he is or what he's doing: I'm wondering if he'll come back home alive or in a body bag.

I turn around to face him. "So you're not signing the divorce papers?"

"I will when I get back, Cal."

"Promise me, Jack."

"Cross my heart and hope to die." He grins like it's all a big joke, then leans down, kisses my cheek, and walks out the door.

I'm still standing at the sink when Elvis sashays through the doggie door. He comes up and presses his cool nose against my legs. It's almost as if he's sniffing out my internal landscape, trying to determine whether to thump his tail and look cute and happy or to press his chunky, warm body against me and offer comfort.

I sit cross-legged on the floor and cuddle his big, square head onto my lap.

"I guess you know your daddy stayed for a while." He licks my hands. "I'm surprised you didn't come back inside to visit."

Elvis gives me his knowing look, the one that says, *Are you kidding? I know when to leave two people alone.*

"Okay. I get it. You're on Jack's side. But you'll have to agree, Champ's a really nice guy."

Most folks would consider talking to a dog to be a sign of something. I don't know what. Probably something unflattering. But dogs are much more highly evolved than you'd think.

When I get off the floor and head upstairs to pack, Elvis trots right along with me. I don't even have to tell him I've decided to take him to the Yucatan. When I drag my bag out of the closet and open it on the floor, Elvis prances over to his toy basket and comes back to drop his favorite chew toy into the suitcase. It's a bedraggled pink dinosaur with both eyes and most of its stuffing missing.

Maybe it's his alter ego. Maybe when Elvis is not dreaming he's the reincarnated King of Rock 'n' Roll, he's dreaming he's a giant brontosaurus that once ruled the earth.

"Listen, Elvis. I know this trip seems hasty, and the tickets will cost me at least four good pairs of designer shoes, but I need some time away to think."

I don't have to tell him what I'm thinking. He knows. When he leans against my legs, it's almost like he's saying, I love you no matter who you choose to be my human daddy.

Elvis' Opinion #2 on Old Bones, New Bones, and 'Dem Bones

For a King used to traveling on his own private jet (the Lisa Marie or Hound Dog II), the flight to the Yucatan was a nightmare akin to bad-movie-review hell. As if starving to death (flying does that to you) and having a bag of stale peanuts tossed at you was not insult enough, try asking for something to wet your whistle. I requested something substantial like Lovie's Prohibition Punch. Instead, the flight attendant brought me a plastic dish of tepid water. It was enough to make me stand up on my lumpy, uncomfortable seat and howl "Treat Me Nice."

I'd have still been howling if Callie hadn't told me I'd have to ride home in the cargo section if I didn't behave myself. If she keeps that up, I'm riding home on the plane with Charlie, Ruby Nell, and Fayrene. (They were on the red-eye that was scheduled to arrive in the Yucatan early this morning.)

Listen, it's a pure relief to set my paws on terra firma and be greeted by Lovie. Now there's a woman after my own heart. Fun is her middle name. She's decked out in black boots with killer heels, a blouse that shows everything she's got—which is plenty, believe me—and enough bangle bracelets to set off every metal detector in the airport.

"I can't wait to show you Rocky's dig." While Lovie holds forth on the romantic potential of Tulum, I hum "What Every Woman Lives For," one of my early hits from 1965.

Now that was the year to fly. Food galore on the plane and your whole family lined up at your gate to make you feel special. These days, it takes an act of God to get through security, and once you do, you feel like you've entered a ghost town filled with robots, everybody hurrying along with briefcases and carry-ons, nobody speaking to anybody else. It's just weird. Makes me long for the old days when a dog was welcome anywhere and could pee on his neighbor's bush without starting a lawsuit.

To get to Tulum, we take a wild taxi ride, then a terrifying journey on the ferry that makes me think I'm going to end up on a Robinson Crusoe adventure, abandoned without silk pillow and Pup-Peroni.

If I ever get off this ferry alive, I'm fixing to start my own archeological dig. Rocky Malone might think he has the corner on unearthing old bones, but he's never seen yours truly in action.

Listen, there's nothing that can comfort a dog like pawing up a good section of dirt and uncovering a good, well-seasoned bone. I don't care if it's an almost-new steak bone or an old ham hock. Just give me some space, let me hum a few bars of " 'Dem Bones," and then stand back and prepare to be amazed.

Chapter 3

Ancient Ruins, Buried Secrets, and Murder

I can see why Lovie calls Tulum "the most romantic spot in the world." High on a cliff, the ruins of the ancient Mayan city overlook the blue-green waters of the Caribbean. Though the structures are squat and unimposing, they are presided over by impressive figures of great winged gods.

Rocky, looking like a dusty, oversized version of Harrison Ford in *Raiders of the Lost Ark*, greets us with bear hugs. Smart man that he is, he has opted for a canvas hat to fend off the beating-down sun instead of Ford's felt fedora.

"Callie, welcome to Tulum." He hangs a possessive arm across Lovie's shoulders.

It doesn't take a rocket scientist to see he's crazy about her. I wish she'd forget her Holy Grail and be thankful for what she has. The first chance I get, I'm going to tell her so.

"Let's stow your luggage and then give you the grand tour." Rocky takes my suitcase and leads me to a small stucco guest cottage on the perimeter of the ancient Mayan ruins.

Inside, he introduces me to Juanita, the housekeeper, who barely looks up from her dusting. A pretty, plump woman I'd guess to be about thirty, she seems extraordinarily shy. I'm going to enjoy getting to know her so she'll be more comfortable around me.

We leave the cottage, and Rocky, still with one arm around Lovie, takes my elbow. "Watch your step. Lots of loose rocks around here."

"Where are Mama and the rest of the gang?"

"They're already exploring." Lovie winks at me. "Fayrene wanted to see the female *difinities*."

Rocky roars with laughter. "Fayrene has her own unique way with words. It took me awhile to catch on that she meant divinities."

"Around Mooreville, we call it *Fayrenese*. To her, a divinity is a candy." I glance at poor Elvis, who seems miserable on his leash. "Is it all right if I turn him loose and let him run a bit? He's been cramped up a long time."

"Sure. Let me call Seth to keep an eye on him." Rocky motions for a young man, as tall and robust as Rocky himself, probably in his late twenties with longish blond hair, then introduces him as Bennett Seth Alford, his second-in-command.

Alford grins when Rocky says, "This is Elvis.

31

Give him some freedom, but make sure he stays out of the roped-off sites."

"You've got it, Rocky."

I instantly like Seth. He has a quick smile and an easy stride that makes you want to pat him on the head, take him home, and invite him to stay for a chicken and dumpling dinner. With his blond good looks and easy manner, he reminds me a bit of Champ.

"Be careful," I tell him. "Elvis is an escape artist."

"Don't worry. I can handle him." Seth takes the leash and walks off whistling. Elvis surprises me by putting his hackles up. Usually, he makes friends with everybody. He's probably out of sorts over the plane ride.

I follow Rocky and Lovie to the Temple of the Frescoes. While Rocky is pointing out the inset panels over the doorways, Uncle Charlie emerges with Mama and Fayrene.

"I'm glad you made it, dear heart." Uncle Charlie gathers me in a paternal hug. "How was the trip?"

"Great." No use telling the unvarnished truth, that I thought the bumpy plane ride was going to dislocate my uterus and totally derail my long-range plans for giving birth. Uncle Charlie worries if anybody in the Valentine family is not happy and well situated.

I always feel better in his company. He's Daddy's only brother, and has been a father to me since I was ten years old—the year my daddy went on to glory land, as folks around Mooreville like to say. Which is nice, when you think about it. The old-fashioned euphemism somehow takes the sting out of death.

"Did you see the driving gods?" Fayrene is in her element, with a green Panama hat to match her cabbage-colored Bermuda shorts and shirt. I mean that in the nicest way. I like cabbage. If it's prepared right.

"The Mayans didn't have cars, Fayrene," Mama says. In a nod to the rocky terrain, she has opted out of her usual rainbow of caftans in favor of denim walking shorts and a fire-engine red tee shirt that I'll have to say sets off her newly brunette look. She reminds me of a seasoned version of one of the glamorous classic movie stars. "Charlie said they're *diving* gods."

"That doesn't make a lick of sense, Ruby Nell. Just look at the size of those cliffs." Fayrene adjusts her hat. Miffed. "You'd have to be a stark raving lunatic to dive around here. You'd break your neck."

"Haven't you ever heard of cliff divers, Fayrene? I'll bet you haven't even opened your guide book."

"I resemble that remark, Ruby Nell. If I'd needed a lecture, I'd have stayed at home with Jarvetis."

"Now, now, dear hearts."

Mama totally ignores Uncle Charlie. She hates to be told what to do. And she won't let a subject drop.

"When I travel to foreign soil, I always try to learn about the culture. I've read my guide book from cover to cover."

"What do you want from me, Ruby Nell? A standing ovulation?"

Rocky's going to wish he'd never invited the Valentines to his dig. I'm about to have a heart attack, but Lovie's eyes are brimming with her effort to hold back laughter.

"I'm fixing to wet my pants." Ordinarily, Lovie would have said pee, but it looks like she's cleaning up her language in deference to her gentleman lover-to-be. "And I think I'm already having a standing ovulation."

I wish she wouldn't encourage Fayrene and Mama. If I had a violent bone in my body, I'd snatch her bald-headed.

Suddenly Fayrene screams. I move to stand in front of Mama in case it's a prelude to some kind of primitive catfight. Or she has spotted a jungle snake.

Instead, Fayrene points behind me. "That basket hound's toting human remains."

She faints dead away. While Mama and Uncle Charlie bend over to revive her, I whirl around to see Elvis prancing toward me with a huge bone in his mouth.

"Holy cow!" If Elvis has destroyed Rocky's archeological site, there goes my welcome.

Bennett Seth Alford is nowhere in sight. So much for watching my dog.

I squat so I can look Elvis straight in the eyes. "Come here, boy."

Instead of obeying, Elvis turns and races toward some old crumbling building that's probably going to cave in any minute and bury him alive. Tulum suddenly loses its glamour.

"Usually he drops anything in his mouth at my feet." Here I am, apologizing for my dog. "Of course, I don't have any treats in my pocket."

Rocky and Uncle Charlie don't hear me. They're already racing off to catch the culprit. The only good thing I can say about this situation is that it broke up a brewing argument between Fayrene and Mama.

What has gotten into them? They might spar a bit, but I've never seen them go this far.

"Lovie, how much Prohibition Punch did Fayrene and Mama have?"

No need to ask if she made any. No matter where Lovie is, she always makes a batch of the punch she calls "the sure cure of everything."

"They wanted to try the tequila."

"Did you forget how Mama acts when she's had tequila? One little drink turns her belligerent."

"Loosen up, Callie. You're in a tropical paradise."

"I'm reserving judgment."

Uncle Charlie returns with Elvis in tow. And right behind him is Rocky, holding onto my dog's prize bone.

"Somebody's going to have to explain this." Rocky holds the bone out for Uncle Charlie's inspection. "Take a look at this femur."

Uncle Charlie takes his time inspecting the bone, and then hands it back to Rocky. "It's too big to be Mayan."

"That's just it, Charlie." Rocky examines the bone more closely. "On a cursory examination, I'd say it's no more than thirty years old."

Relief washes over me. "You mean my dog didn't mess up your dig?"

Rocky pats my shoulder. "Your dog did no harm to the site, Callie. On the other hand, how do you explain this bone?"

"Looks like murder's afoot among the ruins," Mama says, coming over to inspect the bone.

"You don't know that, Mama."

"Did you say murder?" Fayrene, still looking a mite peaked, wobbles over to gander at the bone. "Somebody call the highway control."

Uncle Charlie's already talking on his cell phone to the Mexican authorities.

Listen, I don't care if my dog did dig up the bone. I'm staying as far away from this case as I can get. I've had it with murder. All I want is some peace and quiet and a future baby girl with my dark eyes and Champ's blond hair.

Or black.

Why does Jack always have to ruin my dreams? I'm standing here firmly trying to put him out of my mind when the authorities arrive and drag me right into the middle of the case.

"Señorita, would you mind letting your dog lead us to the site where he found the bone?"

"It's all right, dear heart. I'll take the rest of the ladies inside."

I watch with envy as Uncle Charlie leads Mama, Fayrene, and Lovie into the main cottage, a cool-looking stucco structure where I'm sure Lovie will break out a big pitcher of Prohibition Punch and they'll all sit around retelling this story until it loses its terror and becomes something they can manage, something with a bizarre twist of humor, maybe even something they'll tell next month around the Thanksgiving dinner table.

Laughter through tears: it's the Southern way.

Thank goodness, Rocky stays behind. Having him present is like hiding in the lee of the Rock of Gibraltar.

He pats my shoulder. "I'm right here, Callie."

"Thanks." I kneel beside my dog and rub his ears to let him know finding the new bone is not his fault. "Okay, boy. Show me where you found the bone."

He gives me this basset hound look that says, *You've got to be kidding. I've done my job, let them do theirs.*

"Come on, boy, you can do it. Please. For me."

One of the authorities, a tall man in a tight uniform and a hat that's too small for his big head, rolls his eyes. I'd like to tighten his hatband a notch. That would teach him to disrespect the bond between a good basset and his human mom.

With further coaxing, Elvis finally leads us to a remote spot near the edge of the jungle, far away from the dig. It's creepy here. And the sinking sun doesn't help matters. It's a wonder a big snake didn't pop out of that dangerous-looking jungle growth and swallow my dog whole. Even if he is getting a mite portly.

Out of the corner of my eye, I see Seth coming toward us through the dusk. His color is high and he has the good grace to look apologetic.

"I'm sorry. The dog got away and I couldn't find him."

"That's okay, Seth." Apparently, Rocky is the kind of man who reassures everybody. A wonderful trait in a lover. Or a husband. I make a mental note to tell Lovie.

If I can ever separate myself from murder.

"Is it okay if I go now?"

The man in the too-tight hat nods, and Rocky says, "Do you want me to escort you back, Callie?"

"No, thanks. You stay here. I have Elvis."

When I get back to the cottage, everybody

starts talking at once. I sink into a rattan chair and the comfort of familiar voices and beloved faces, grateful that the investigation afoot has nothing to do with me.

Dinner is served alfresco by a tall, skinny woman Rocky introduces as Rosita, Juanita's twin. They're nothing alike. While Juanita is all curves, Rosita is all sharp bones with a face like a hatchet. And she's so taciturn, she won't even answer when you ask her a direct question.

Where did Rocky find this woman? She gives me the creeps.

It's a relief when the long day finally ends and I can head toward my bedroom.

The Mexican authorities have taken the femur as well as the rest of the human remains they dug up, Uncle Charlie is out for an evening stroll with Mama, and Fayrene is on the phone with Jarvetis.

"The bone was as big as my leg, hon, and the head honcho heading up this infestation looked like General Cluster."

For once, Fayrene hit the nail on the head. *Infestation* is exactly how this entire investigative mess feels. Though how Fayrene has a clue about General Custer's looks is beyond me.

I wave good night, then proceed down a narrow, tiled hallway to my room. Tomorrow I'm sure Fayrene's version of *Murder Among the Ruins* will be all over Mooreville's grapevine.

I could be sad that I don't have anybody to call but I pride myself on being independent. To tell the truth, though, I do have somebody, but if I call Champ, he'll worry and want to hop on the next plane. Part of the reason I'm down here is so I can do some heavy thinking about having a future with him.

When I push open the door to my bedroom, I startle Juanita.

"Sorry, señorita." She blushes. "I was doing the dusting."

Before I can say *thank you,* she scuttles out.

"That's strange," I say, and Elvis thumps his tail in agreement. "She was dusting when I met her hours ago. How long does it take to dust?"

My dog's grisly discovery has me spooked. I'll feel better after I've showered and put on my pajamas. There's something about the end of the day that always soothes me.

Grabbing my toiletries and pajamas, I head across the hall, take a long soak, then return to my guest room. It's little more than a cubicle with tiled floors, sparsely furnished with a bed, a nightstand, and a slatted wooden bench with three hooks for my clothes. Somehow this minimalism comforts me. Nothing excessive to clutter the mind.

"Good night, Elvis."

He's already sprawled on his pink satin doggie pillow. Call me silly, but I couldn't bear the thought of him having to sleep on a bare floor so I packed his pillow. Loyal companions deserve the best.

He thumps his tail and makes a series of grunts, dog speak for *I love you.*

At least I tell myself that's what he's saying. Listen, I know he's only a dog, but one thing I can be sure of: he'll never leave me for a Harley. Or for any other reason.

The moon coming through my window is gorgeous, but even the lure of a romantic Mayan moon can't entice me out of this bed.

"Callie?" I nearly jump through the ceiling. Lovie's standing in my doorway in a nightgown that would barely cover a sneeze. "Are you awake?"

"I am now."

"Good." She switches on the light, and plops onto my bed. "I need to talk."

"Good grief, Lovie. You walked across the compound like that? Why didn't you put on some clothes?"

"I want to be ready when Rocky comes back."

"Where is he?"

"Off with that awful old man who guards the digs. Morgan something or other. They found some ancient pottery pieces today." She says a word shocking enough to cause earth tremors. "I wish he'd get that excited about my piece."

"Good grief, Lovie."

"Well, I do."

"Give him time. He strikes me as the kind of man who likes to move slowly."

"I'd prefer not to be in a wheelchair and Depends when he finally locates my Holy Grail."

"Forget about your Holy Grail. Just enjoy getting to know him."

"That's not what Fayrene and Aunt Ruby Nell told me."

"What did they tell you?"

"How did you know you were in love with Jack?"

"You're deliberately changing the subject. That makes me nervous, Lovie."

"You didn't answer my question."

"I'm not in love with Jack." I don't think. Am I? What a disaster.

"You were once. How did you know?"

I wish I could roll over and pull the sheets over my head. But this is my cousin who plies me with chocolate because she thinks I'm too skinny, brings me *I Love Lucy* reruns when she thinks I need to laugh, arms us with tissues and buttered popcorn when I need to cry, and never, ever tells me I'm foolish or cowardly or silly no matter how foolish or cowardly or silly I act.

I get up, take a six-pack of Hershey's Chocolate Kisses with almonds out of my suitcase, then climb back into bed. Lovie grabs a handful and starts peeling golden wrappers.

"It started with his smile, Lovie. And the way he laughs. And his hands. He has these incredibly beautiful hands, smooth olive skin with curved thumbs. I never tired of touching his thumbs."

Lovie nods and unwraps more chocolates while I keep talking. No matter how painful it is to remember.

It's not the easy things you do that make a friendship. It's the hard ones.

Chapter 4

Sandy Beaches, Small Umbrellas, and Big Problems

The next morning I join Mama, Uncle Charlie, and Fayrene in the little courtyard at the back of the main cottage. Though Mama's looking chipper in a bright yellow tee shirt, and Fayrene's neon green outfit lights up everything within six feet, I can tell something is amiss. Even Uncle Charlie looks a little flustered.

"What's wrong?" I pull out my chair, pour myself a big glass of orange juice, and put a flaky looking croissant on my plate. Thank goodness Rosita is nowhere in sight. If there was ever a person who can spoil your appetite, she's the one.

"Nothing to concern us, dear heart. But I think

it best if we leave for Cozumel today. Rocky's going to be busy trying to carry on his work while the Mexican authorities are here."

Does Uncle Charlie know something about the bones Elvis discovered that he's not telling us? That would be highly likely. When we were in the middle of the Bubbles Caper, and even the Elvis impersonator fiasco, I used to wonder how Uncle Charlie could find out important information even before the police. Now I know. He was once an operative in The Company, and he's the main reason Jack's there today.

A lesser woman might resent him for that, but this is my Uncle Charlie we're talking about—the heart, soul, and backbone of the Valentine family, the quiet, steady man who dispenses hugs, great advice, and wisdom couched in quotes from Shakespeare. As far as I'm concerned, he can do no wrong.

"We'll leave today," he adds.

"It can't be soon enough for me." Lovie marches into the courtyard, snatches up my juice, and drinks it in one gulp.

"Holy cow, Lovie. I'd have poured you some."

"I'm looking for instant gratification. And Rocky's too busy digging up old bones to jump mine."

"Now, now, dear heart. You should stay here and help your nice young fellow."

"Rocky doesn't need my help, Daddy. With anything." Lovie grabs my croissant, and proceeds to eat it like I'm not sitting there with an empty plate.

While I'm serving myself again, Mama, Uncle Charlie, and Fayrene head inside to pack.

"What in the world is wrong with you, Lovie? Uncle Charlie's right. Rocky needs you."

"Not enough to find the national treasure." She helps herself to another croissant. Thankfully not from my plate. "Besides, distance makes the heart grow fonder. I'm going to give him a few days to pine for me."

"I don't think that's a good idea. But who am I to give love advice?"

"Exactly."

"That was tacky, Lovie."

"I'm a tacky, shallow person."

"You're not. Just impulsive. And headstrong. And bossy."

She throws her second roll at me. But only after she takes a big bite.

The only good thing I can say about Lovie's leaving Rocky today is that she won't have time to implement Mama's seduction strategy.

Our hotel in Cozumel is right on the water, and Lovie heads straight for the beach. I'm torn between going shopping with Mama and Fayrene, who have a hankering to check out the

Mexican silver, and chasing after Lovie, who has a penchant for trouble.

Lovie wins. By the time I can get Elvis properly watered and walked, she's already sprawled in a lounge chair collecting umbrellas. The tiny paper kind that come in those tall drinks that have enough tequila—and no telling what else—to knock out a three hundred pound elephant.

"Lovie, how many of those have you had?"

"Who's counting? Besides, I'm in mourning."

"For what?"

"The death of Rocky's libido."

"I'm sure that's not true, Lovie."

"How else would you explain his failure to succumb to the most voluptuous caterer in Mississippi? I've a good mind to march back over there and give him a piece of my mind."

"It'll be hard to march to Tulum unless you can walk on water."

"If you're not careful, you're going to turn into a smartass like me."

"If you care to remember, we crossed on the ferry."

Lovie shades her eyes and sticks out her tongue. "Pull up a chair, Callie. Get a tan. Get a drink. And get another one for me, too."

"Just one. And then we should walk a bit and see the island. I noticed some really neat shops down at the pier. What's the drink called?"

"Tropical Double Trouble."

"Why am I not surprised?"

I head to the small beach bar and order two drinks.

"Go light on the tequila," I say.

The bartender grins, which could mean anything from *okay* to *I don't understand a word you're saying* to *forget it*.

I think it meant the last one because the drink tastes suspiciously strong.

"Hmmm, good." Lovie pulls her sunglasses down and peers at me over the rims. "Do you think Rocky's in love with Juanita?"

"He can't even look at anybody but you, Lovie. Why on earth would you say that?"

"Because she's in love with him. You ought to see the way she acts around Rocky. Like some lovesick puppy." She pats Elvis. "No offense, pal."

"Even if the maid is in love with him, Rocky's not a player."

"Rosita's in love with him, too. The twin tarts. You ought to see the way they make eyes at him."

"You've got to be kidding. The cook? She's too severe to love herself, let alone Rocky."

"If they keep on flirting with my man, I'm going to send them back where they came from in tar and feathers."

"I think you've had too much to drink, Lovie."

"I don't think you've had enough."

"Maybe you're right. But no more of that silly talk, please. I want to relax and watch the water."

By the time I've finished my drink, I'm almost too sleepy to stand up and shop for shoes. But the sun has not set, the market is nearby, and I have a deep need to soothe my sagging spirits.

I place my tiny paper umbrella on the table beside Lovie's collection. She's already half asleep and Elvis is snoozing beside her chair.

"Lovie, do you mind keeping an eye on Elvis? I think I'll try to find Fayrene and Mama. And maybe a cute pair of espadrilles."

"Go on. Relax, enjoy." She gives me a lazy wave without even opening her eyes.

"You're sure you'll be all right?"

"If I were any better, they'd have to throw a parade in my honor."

I pet my dog, tell him to watch after my cousin, then head back across the beach. When I reach the sidewalk, I look back to see Lovie and Elvis right where I left them, snoozing in the sun.

I head toward the market on the pier, but not without the niggling feeling that something is amiss. What, I don't know. Maybe it's something back home.

I pull out my cell phone and call Champ.

"Callie, how wonderful to hear your voice. How are you?"

Our connection is surprisingly good. He sounds like he's around the corner instead of in Mississippi.

"I'm good." My next thought is to ask about my animals, but shouldn't I have something more to talk about with Champ than the care and feeding of seven stray cats? Well, they're not so stray since I gave them names. Still . . . "How's the weather back home?"

Oh, great. Now that's a subject for lovers.

Except we're not lovers. Yet. Just potential with a capital *P.*

"Splendid. I took Hoyt for a romp and six of your Seven Dwarf cats are lolling in the gazebo in the sunshine. Happy is chasing butterflies."

"She's so cute."

"All your pets are healthy, happy, and well adjusted. You're a good animal mother, Callie."

"Thanks, Champ. I feel like you've given me a mother-of-the-year award."

There's a silence on his end. "You know I want children, Callie. I hope you'll think about my proposal while you're gone."

"I will. I promise."

"Good. I'd like a *yes* when you get back, but I won't pressure you. I know you still have legal work to finish with Jack."

I wish he hadn't mentioned my almost-ex's name. It's impossible to think about Jack in the same sentence as a proposal from Luke

Champion without feeling like I'm being squeezed in a lemonade press.

"Listen, I have to go, Champ. Lovie's in charge of Elvis, and I don't want to leave her too long."

Which is not exactly a lie.

I hurry along the water's edge, admiring the huge Carnival cruise ship docked at the pier. The shops are clustered in a small grouping at the end of the long pier so tourists can't help but spill into the market.

I go into the first shop I find and come out with a little pair of yellow espadrilles that will look great with my favorite sundress. Feeling like a better human being, I meander among the Mexican silver and Mayan masks until I find Uncle Charlie.

As usual, he's patiently waiting for Mama (and Fayrene, of course). They're inside a shop that sells everything from faux Mayan pottery to real island tequila, of all things. Naturally, Mama is looking at the tequila.

I sit on a wooden bench outside the store beside Uncle Charlie. "Maybe I ought to go in there and steer Mama toward something else."

"Let her have her fun. She hasn't had that much fun since Michael died."

That's a new twist for me. I think of Mama's escapades as nothing but fun. Apparently Uncle Charlie is seeing something I don't, a deep sense of loss that underlies Mama's cheerful, zany façade, a lifelong yearning for the man she loved and lost. My father. Michael Valentine. The man I've heard her call "the love of my life."

I lean my head against the cool stucco of the building, gaze across the turquoise waters of the Caribbean, and let myself slide into the deep relaxation that comes from being far away from home. Lovie and Elvis are sleeping on the beach, Mama and Fayrene are in shoppers' paradise, and Uncle Charlie is content.

What could possibly go wrong?

Elvis' Opinion #3 on Bad Auras, Foolhardy Plans, and Rescue Missions

When a shadow blocks my sun, I am rudely awakened from my nap. As if depriving a deserving dog of his sleep weren't bad enough, the man who is making the shadow gets every one of my hackles up. Listen, don't tell me a dog can't read auras. And this man's is blacker than the pits of Hades. I'd as soon chew his leg off as look at him.

Out of deference to the Valentine family, I refrain. Listen, you're looking at a former icon in a dog suit who has adoring fans around the world. I know how to put on a public face.

When Mr. Dark Aura starts flirting with Lovie, I just put my brilliant head on my paws and play dumb.

"Hello, gorgeous," he tells her.

Lovie's collected so many umbrellas she can barely see him, let alone see through him even if he is wearing aviator sunglasses and a black wig I'd bury in the backyard.

I'm not letting this dude out of my sight.

With my mismatched ears, I can pick up trouble a mile away, and believe me, this jerk has me growling "T-R-O-U-B-L-E."

Lovie puts her hand on my neck, then shades her eyes and looks up at the rude intruder with her coy, come-on expression. Granted, she's feeling rejected and he's good-looking. And just her type. Or at least the type she was attracted to before she fell for Rocky Malone.

But can't she see who he is? I try warning her with a low-voiced rendition of the "Devil in Disguise," but she just keeps on responding to his heavy-handed flirtation.

Before I know what's happening, Lovie's rising from her lounge chair and staggering off with this dapper dude. Callie's nowhere in sight and Charlie's off with Ruby Nell and Fayrene. If this sleazy rake thinks I'm going to watch Lovie leave with nothing more than a "Vaya Con Dios," he's barking up the wrong tree.

I wait until they're down the beach far enough for him to think I'm still happily lazing in the sun, then I shag my ample butt into gear and take off after them.

It's up to me to save the day.

Just my luck, he's taking Lovie to the ferry. But if you think a little thing like seasickness and visions of being stranded in shark-infested waters would stop a dog of my caliber, you'd be wrong. Listen, mess with my people, you're liable to come up missing a body part.

Now, sneaking aboard a ferry might stymie lesser dogs like that goofy Lhasa apso upstart back at Hair.Net or that silly shih tzu down the street from Callie, but it's easy for a clever basset to slip between the legs of milling tourists. Once I'm safely onboard, I find a nice cool spot in the shade of a man the size of twin oak tree trunks, and flop down to reconnoiter.

The ferry gets underway, and I watch Lovie leaning over the railing losing her Tropical Double Troubles. She looks close to passing out. The man she's running off with hands her his handkerchief and acts concerned.

Concerned, my crooked hind leg. He may act like "The Love Machine," but he doesn't have a clue that a clever "Roustabout" is lurking in the shadows.

If he makes one false move, I'm liable to get dangerous. And I'm not talking about my usual modus operandi of bringing women and French poodles to a screaming, fainting frenzy.

Bring it on, dude. There's nothing a dog of my intelligence and savoir faire can't handle.

Chapter 5

Missing Person, Dire Predictions, and Arkansas Razorbacks

By the time I get back to my room at the Cozumel Palace, I'd like nothing better than to sink into the Jacuzzi. But there's no sign of Lovie and Elvis, so I head to the beach to look for them.

Lovie is probably cooked to a crisp by now, and there's no telling what my dog is up to. As much as I'd like to simply stand and admire the colors of the sunset across the water, I hurry along to retrieve part of the missing Valentine contingent.

Our party is meeting for dinner tonight at the semi-elegant MoMoNoHaHa restaurant. It's a good thing it's in our hotel. If Lovie had any more Tropical Double Troubles, she'll be in no condition to walk far.

I'm wearing my new espadrilles, so I scan the beach hoping to spot Lovie and Elvis, then simply call and wave them to come in. Alas, they're nowhere in sight. Which means I'm either at the wrong spot (highly unlikely) or they've moved to another spot.

If I were Lovie, I'd say a bad word. I'm supposed to meet the family for dinner in less than an hour. Now is no time to play hide-and-seek with my cousin.

I dial her cell phone, and leave a voice mail. "Lovie, where in the world are you? Is Elvis with you? Call me. We're supposed to meet for dinner." Then I pull off my shoes and set off across the sand, calling my dog.

You haven't lived till you've strolled a foreign beach yelling, "Elvis!" Most of the sun worshippers have gone inside, but the ones who are left turn to stare at me as if they can't decide whether I've gone crazy or I'm convinced Elvis never died and I spend all my free time searching the world for him.

Listen, let them jeer. I'll do just about anything to find my dog.

"Elvis, where are you, boy? Come here."

"Don't expect too much, lady." The hunky stranger is watching me, deadpan. I can't tell whether he's making fun or is an aspiring wag. "Last I saw, he was up at the bar having a Tropical Double Trouble."

I don't even stop to explain that Elvis is a dog. There's no telling what he'd say to that.

Giving the smart-mouth hunk a wide circuit, I continue my search. I believe in keeping the body healthy, so it doesn't take me long to make a quick tour of Cozumel Palace's beachfront. Lovie and Elvis are nowhere to be found.

They were probably doubling back when I

came outside. Most likely, Lovie's in the Jacuzzi and up to her neck in bubbles this very minute. And Elvis is probably ensconced on his satin pillow for the night.

I turn and head back. To an empty suite. No Lovie hogging the hot tub. No Elvis thumping his tail on the floor.

If I have one fault, it's being a worrier. But Lovie's grown and Elvis would never wander far from me. I refuse to spoil the evening imagining the worst. Lovie probably stopped in a cute little sidewalk café and lost track of time.

I take a quick shower, slide into a darling pair of gold-and-bronze Ferragamo sandals and a short pink silk dress, then call home.

"Hi, Darlene. How are things going?" I make my voice so perky it could brew coffee. I don't want her to think I'm checking up on her.

"Fabulous! Trixie Moffett is now officially engaged to Roy Jessup." (He's the owner of Mooreville Feed and Seed, the third anchor of Mooreville society after Gas, Grits, and Guts and Hair.Net.) "Roy wants to hold the reception at his farm supply store."

"Trixie must be a basket case."

"She was hotter than a pistol. She wanted me to paint her nails seashell pink to take her mind off his silly notions."

"Good. She loves pink polish."

"I didn't paint her nails that wimpy pink. Her

horoscope said she was due for a dramatic change. It took a lot of persuasion and two cups of Prohibition Punch, but I finally talked her into going with neon Texas Bluebonnet."

Holy cow! I wonder if I was hasty in my choice of manicurists. I'd head home on the next plane if I could find Lovie and Elvis.

"How did Trixie feel about her blue nails?"

"The horoscope is always right. She loved them, natch."

Good grief. Shades of Fayrene. I assume *natch* means *naturally.*

"Are you sure Trixie was satisfied? I pride myself on always pleasing my clients."

"Oh, I threw in some daisy art with cute little rhinestone centers for free. If Trixie had been any more pleased when she left here, she'd have popped right out of her trashy bustier."

"Good grief! You didn't call Trixie *trashy* to her face, did you?"

I don't know whether Darlene's laugh means she did or she didn't. By the time I get back to Mooreville, I'm liable not to have a single customer left.

"Now, Callie, don't you worry about a thing. I've got it all covered."

Darlene's reassurance does not ease my mind.

Plus, Elvis and Lovie still haven't come back. I try to reach her again, without any luck, and then call Rocky to see if she decided to carry through her threat to go over there and give him a piece of her mind.

"I don't want to alarm you, Rocky," I say, which probably does just the opposite. "Have you heard from Lovie?"

"Not since she left."

"She's not in Tulum?"

"I thought she was with you."

"Well, she is. Sort of."

"What do you mean?"

"She was here this afternoon. At the beach. But she hasn't come back to the room and it's time to meet Uncle Charlie for dinner."

"Lovie's not the most punctual person I know. And she's extraordinarily independent. She probably wandered off downtown and lost track of time."

"I'm sure that's it, Rocky."

"Call me when she gets back."

I promise Rocky to call, then race off and get all turned around trying to find the HaHaHeeHee or whatever it is. Sense of direction is not my strong suit, especially when I'm inside a cavernous hotel and can't use the sun to tell east from west.

Why can't life be as simple here as it is in Mooreville where there's only one restaurant? And it has a name that's friendly and easy to remember. No frills. No airs. Just Linda and Til's.

A big billboard out front—EAT—visible to everybody driving to Mantachie and points north on Highway 371.

When I finally find the restaurant, it's my full intention to put on a smile and enjoy dinner. After all, Lovie's a grown woman.

Besides, I pride myself on not being a party pooper. But one look at my face, and Uncle Charlie sniffs trouble. All it takes is one question, "What's wrong, dear heart?" and I'm spilling my worried guts all over the NoHeHoHo.

"Lord, help us." Fayrene jumps straight out of her chair. "Lovie's been hijacked."

If Mama hadn't tugged Fayrene's hunter green tunic, she might have levitated. Hijacked. Kidnapped. What does it matter? They're both awful.

"Let's not get alarmed, dear hearts. If I need to, I'll call Jack."

I sincerely hope not. I'm trying to get away from Jack, not run into him at every corner, especially in what could be the most romantic spot in the world. If it weren't for Elvis digging up suspicious bones and Lovie turning up missing . . .

Why would Uncle Charlie be talking about calling Jack on such a short absence, anyhow? It can mean only one thing: he knows stuff he's keeping from us. Probably stuff that would give me nightmares and make Lovie say a word that would get her on the prayer list at Wildwood Baptist Church back home.

If she were anywhere around to say that word.

I sink into my chair. "Elvis is missing, too."

"I don't know about the rest of you, but I'm starved." Mama signals the waiter. "I'm ordering dinner."

"That's callous, Mama."

"All of you are overreacting." Mama orders a carafe of Pinot Grigio, then sends the waiter off to give us time to study the menu. "It's not unusual for Lovie to go off to enjoy a small diversion without telling anybody. If she doesn't show up tonight, she'll probably show up in the morning wondering why we all made such a fuss."

"You're right, dear heart. Let's enjoy our meal."

"Bobby predicted this." Fayrene takes a fortifying sip of her wine. "When I talked to Jarvetis today, Bobby was there checking out the séance room. He predicted danger from a dark-eyed stranger."

"He always predicts danger from a dark-eyed stranger," Uncle Charlie says. "Now, here comes the waiter. Let's enjoy the meal. 'All's well that ends well.'"

I don't know why, but when Uncle Charlie quotes Shakespeare, we all feel reassured. Plus, he keeps the talk away from missing persons and turns it toward the size of the undertakers' convention.

"It's going to be a big one this year," he says.

Mama agrees. "On the way to dinner, I met Lovie's old boyfriend checking in."

"Who?" I ask. It's hard to keep up with Lovie's old boyfriends. She has as many ex-lovers as I have satisfied customers at Hair.Net. And believe me, that's a lot.

"Alvin Farkle. The undertaker from Arkansas."

If I remember correctly, that relationship ended badly, which is totally unlike Lovie's other breakups. She's such a lively, charming, and forthright woman, it's hard for anybody to have hard feelings for her, even the men she used to dump with the regularity of a Greyhound bus on its daily run to Memphis.

"I'll bet undertakers will be here from every one of the contingency states."

Trust Fayrene. You can always count on her for laughs and plenty of gossip. But, I have to say that by the time I leave the NoMoreHeHeHe, I'm feeling much less stressed about Lovie and Elvis. In fact, I fully expect to see them waiting for me in the room.

Alas, the lights are off and the room is empty. I try Lovie's cell phone again, but this time I don't even get voice mail, just that awful message that the person I'm trying to reach is unavailable, a surefire guarantee that I'm in for a sleepless night.

• • •

An earsplitting Arkansas Razorback *soooeeee!* jolts me upright. It takes a minute for me to realize that I'm in bed at the posh Cozumel Palace, the clock hands on the luminous dial are pointing to the crack of eight a.m., and I have barely slept three hours. After a restless night of worry and nightmares with my eyes wide open, I'm in no mood to be deprived of anything by loud guests throwing a hoedown in the next room.

Another loud *soooeee* splits the air.

I pride myself on tolerance, but one more yell for the Arkansas home team and I'll be reaching for the telephone.

I lie back down and pull the sheet over my face, but no sooner does my head touch the pillow than a loud knock jerks me out of bed. Holy cow! Somebody has found Lovie and Elvis bound and gagged. Or worse: Dead.

I turn on the lamp, give my bleary eyes time to adjust, then grab my robe and head to the door. Rocky's there, looking sleep deprived and worried.

"Callie, I'm sorry to wake you. But I took the early ferry over. I haven't heard a word from Lovie. Have you?"

"Not yet. That's why I didn't call." I don't think Mama's suggestion that Lovie is out seeking diversion would reassure Rocky, so I keep my mouth shut about that. "Come in. I'll make us some coffee."

"I hate to intrude." Ever the perfect gentleman, Rocky hesitates to enter my bedroom, but when I motion, he comes inside.

While I find the filters and set about brewing coffee in the two-cup coffeemaker, Rocky sinks into one of the twin chairs in the window nook.

"I've tried repeatedly to reach her." He pulls out his cell phone and tries again. "No luck, Callie."

As if his face hadn't said it all. If my nerves were stretched any tighter I'd be twanging like an upright piano in a country and western bar.

"Lovie's not an early riser, Rocky."

"I've noticed."

"She could show up at any time."

I can tell he doesn't believe me. I don't even believe myself.

"The Mexican police are all over Tulum. It seems the bones your dog found solved a thirty-year mystery."

"Not murder, I hope."

"It's too early to tell. But the case hit home. The bones belong to Lucille Morgan, the wife of the guard at Tulum."

"One of your men?"

"Not technically. Archie Morgan guards my site, but he came with the territory. He's American, but he's been at Tulum for thirty-five years. Five years after he arrived in the Yucatan, his wife vanished without a trace."

This news makes me weak-kneed. I prop myself against the wall, hoping the smell of coffee dripping into the carafe will revive me.

"Rocky, you don't think Lovie's disappearance is connected to the disappearance of that woman, do you?"

A loud pounding at my door, followed by a series of *yahoos* and *woohoos* brings conversation to a standstill. I hurry to see who's making such an unholy commotion.

It's Fayrene, standing in the hallway in a zucchini-colored bathrobe with her hair twisted in lettuce green foam curlers and covered with a hairnet the color of seasickness. Any other time I'd offer beauty advice. But between the sight of all that green and my worry about Lovie and Elvis, I've lost my desire to tell her that those rubber rollers are going to put tacky kinks in her hair and make her look old.

Before I can say *come in,* Fayrene brushes past me and plops into the chair beside Rocky. Belatedly, I think how unusual it is for her to be gadding about in her bathrobe. She has a green outfit for every occasion, and she's usually meticulous about the way she dresses.

"If you've got any vodka in that wet bar, you might as well get it out. You're going to need it."

"Holy cow, Fayrene. What's wrong now?"

"Lovie's been hijacked."

Rocky looks puzzled. "Do you mean kidnapped?"

"That's what I said."

"How do you know?"

I was just about to ask the same question, though I could tell Rocky that Fayrene is the first one in the know when there's breaking news.

"While Ruby Nell was getting her beauty sleep, I decided to go downstairs and conduct my own little infestation. And you'll never guess what I found out over the monumental breakfast."

Rocky is looking slightly shell-shocked. I don't have time to interpret *investigation* and *continental.*

"If she was kidnapped, time is important," I tell her.

She gets up and takes her time pouring a cup of coffee. Next to Mama, Fayrene is the biggest drama queen I know. Only my deeply ingrained Southern manners and my natural good nature keep me from screaming and snatching her bald-headed.

Rocky seems to be relying on the same combination of social graces.

"There was a woman from Arkansas picking over the crème-filled doughnuts. She toured Tulum late yesterday afternoon, and remembers seeing a woman who fits Lovie's description on the ferry going over."

"Lovie never arrived," Rocky says.

"If you'll hold onto your socks, I'm getting to that part. The woman said that when Lovie left the ferry, she was being absconded by a man."

"Escorted?" Rocky pulls one ear like his hearing is going bad.

"That's what I said."

"Did she describe him?" I ask.

"She said she was so busy wondering why Lovie was wearing nothing but a swimsuit with a cover-up, she couldn't remember the man."

"Was Elvis with them?"

"I asked, but the woman said she thought he was dead."

I think I'm going to scream. "Did you tell her Elvis is a basset hound?"

"No. I thought everybody knew Elvis."

I need to talk to this woman. "What was her name, Fayrene?"

"Lula. No, Lola. Wait a minute. It was Lulu. Lulu Farkle."

I'd ask if Lulu was any relation to Lovie's old boyfriend, Alvin, but I don't want to upset Rocky any more than he already is. He's taking all this news very hard.

There's only one cup of coffee left, and I pour it for him.

"Lovie knows how to take care of herself." I guess I'm trying to reassure both of us. "Besides, she's been gone little more than twelve hours. It's too soon to panic."

Nobody in this room believes my bald-faced lie. Least of all, me. I walk over to the nightstand, pick up my cell phone, and hit number three on my speed dial.

One ring, and Uncle Charlie is on the line.

"Rocky is here, Uncle Charlie. We need to talk."

Within fifteen minutes Uncle Charlie and Mama are in my room, and all of us are discussing the latest developments.

Who coaxed Lovie off the beach and why? And where is Elvis?

Elvis' Opinion #4 on Kidnapped, Hoodwinked, and Hoodooed

By now Callie is worried sick about me, and all the Valentines will be wondering what has happened to Lovie. If I could leave and get back on that ferry to Cozumel, I could tell them a thing or two. But I'm dealing with a life-and-death situation here.

While Lovie was passed out, she got blindfolded and trussed up like a Thanksgiving turkey, and I'm hunkered down outside the primitive jungle shack where she's being held. Listen, this place is not fit for a mole, let alone the national treasure and a dog of my exalted status.

If this were one of my many movies, I'd race

inside with all my hackles up and snatch Lovie from the jaws of death, but I know better. Only "Fools Rush In." Trust me. While Lovie's coming to, I'm watching and waiting for the perfect moment to be the hero that I am.

With my eagle eyes peering through a crack and my mismatched ears on radar, I don't miss a trick.

"Where are we?" Lovie says to the devil who led her off the boat. She giggles, which means she's still sloshed and doesn't have the faintest clue who she's with or why, let alone the kind of danger we're in.

The dirty rotten rat who brought her here leans down to make sure her ropes are secure.

Lovie giggles again. "Rocky, is that you? If you like *kinky,* why didn't you tell me so? You didn't have to pull this kidnapping stunt."

Well, bless'a my soul. This is worse than I thought. She is not only clueless about the danger she's in, but she thinks she's been prepped for fun and games with bondage.

If he messes with her, he'll have me to answer to. Nobody steals the honor of a Valentine while I'm around. I'll roll over him like the "Wabash Cannonball"—a great song I rehearsed for a 1974 performance in Vegas but never got around to recording. Too bad. I'd have turned it platinum.

But leaving memory lane and back to the

disaster at hand—I'd go into that primitive shack right now and show that lowdown skunk how a dog of my status takes care of business, but that would be jumping the gun. First I've got to come up with a plan. It's one thing to put this dude behind bars and have him singing the "Jailhouse Rock," but it's another to make sure Lovie is safe.

Besides, if I tip my hand now, I'm liable to end up crooning "Release Me."

This is no small man we're dealing with. He's got the build of somebody who lifts weights and could bench-press Texas.

Fortunately, I don't have to resort to fisticuffs. In addition to being so famous I had to take the service elevator after my shows to keep from being mobbed by fans, I'm a superior dog-detective. If I could evade fans in my other life as a world-famous entertainer and catch killers right and left in this one as a famous man reincarnated in a dog suit, I can certainly outsmart this dude.

Fortunately the captor is not interested in bondage. While Lovie's still trying to get his mojo working, he's rummaging in her purse, stealing her cell phone so she can't call for help. Not that she's in any shape to. Plus, he's taking her driver's license and credit cards so she can't be identified.

"Rocky, answer me." Lovie struggles upright on her cot. "Why are you acting like this?"

"Lie down and shut up."

For a minute she goes still, and then she bucks around and tries to kick him right where it hurts most. She would have, too, if he hadn't sidestepped and if she weren't bound tighter than a mummy.

The big snake puts Lovie's possessions into his pocket, then slithers out the door, leaving her to moan "A Mess of Blues."

And I'm not talking about a song that in my other life as a musical icon in a sequined jumpsuit I turned into gold.

I scuttle behind some bushes till the mean dude is out of sight. After he vanishes into the thick jungle growth, Lovie and I are left with nothing for company except a few noisy parrots and obnoxious monkeys.

Forget that parrots can say, *Polly wants a cracker,* and monkeys can do a few tricks. I'd be in "Heartbreak Hotel" if I had to count on them for help.

It's up to me to save the day.

Chapter 6

Bad Boy, Bad Wind, and Big Trouble

It's barely the crack of nine and everybody is still gathered in my bedroom having a summit conference over Lovie. Fayrene keeps repeating her discoveries over the "monumental" breakfast and talking about hijacking, Rocky's getting more agitated by the minute, and I'm about to fall to pieces in my bathrobe with my hair uncombed.

Mama is the only one keeping her cool.

"I think we're all jumping the gun. Lovie and Elvis haven't even been gone twenty-four hours. Any minute I expect her to walk through that door and laugh at all of us."

Does Mama really believe that, or is she only trying to reassure us? Ordinarily, I view Mama as somebody who puts herself at the center of the universe, but since my conversation with Uncle Charlie at the pier, I'm seeing her in a different light.

Too, there were all those moments during my childhood, after Daddy died, when Mama would swoop into my bedroom where I was moping, grab my hands, drag me into the living room, and start singing, "Side by Side." Back then I wondered how she could be so cheerful when all I wanted to do was mourn, but now I see her antics were her attempt to make me feel better.

And she did. But now, I'm older and wiser. With the newly found bones of Tulum turning out to be the remains of a long-vanished woman, a whole new layer of horrible possibilities has been added to Lovie's disappearance.

If she's connected to an old mystery, the big question is why?

If she were here, we'd have our heads together trying to connect the dots. Though Lovie looks and sometimes acts frivolous, that's a façade. Like Mama, she loves to play for laughs. I'd think that was a common Valentine gene, but I don't have it.

Maybe I'm too serious. Maybe if I lived more for kicks, I wouldn't be here in the Yucatan with a missing cousin and a pending divorce. I'd be home with a husband who never left. The biggest things on my mind would be bringing *Vogue* hairstyles to Mooreville and getting pregnant.

Of course, Jack never wanted any children. Which is the root of our problem.

"I'm calling Jack." Uncle Charlie whips out his cell phone. Is he reading minds now?

I'm torn between relief and dismay. If anybody can find Lovie and Elvis, it's Jack. Still, the idea of being thrown together with him in the most romantic setting in the world is unnerving. To say the least.

"That's a great idea, Charlie," Mama says.

I'd be surprised at her quick turnaround from "let's not worry" to "let's call in the troops" if I didn't know her motive. She wants Jack and me back together. And not because of grandchildren. She thinks he's my soul mate, and she'll seize any opportunity to promote reconciliation.

It won't work. As far as I'm concerned, Jack's

a bad boy blowing in on a bad wind. I plan to stay as far away from him as possible.

As soon as Uncle Charlie's briefed Jack and is off the phone, Mama asks, "What did Jack say?"

"He's on his way." That could take awhile. For all we know, Jack's in China. "He'll be here in forty-five minutes."

"Forty-five minutes! Where is he?"

"He happens to be on a little holiday down here." Uncle Charlie gives me a warning look. Belatedly, I remember that neither Fayrene nor Mama knows Jack's true profession.

"That figures." I try for nonchalance, but anybody with an eye for a lie would catch me. "He'd view the Yucatan as a huge playground."

"He would not," Mama says. "Personally, I feel better knowing he's coming."

Leave it to her to defend Jack. Though to be honest, he never did act like a playboy—if you don't count that big Harley Screamin' Eagle with the heated seats. Now there's a toy for a player if I ever saw one.

"Now, dear hearts, let's keep to the matter at hand. If anybody can find Lovie, it's Jack."

"Why Jack?" Rocky's question is valid. "Why not a private eye?"

If you didn't know Jack's profession—and nobody here does except Uncle Charlie and me—why would you think he'd be the one to solve the mystery?

"He did a brief stint at the police academy before he became an international business consultant," Uncle Charlie says.

Jack never spent one day of his life at the police academy. But, considering that Uncle Charlie used to work for The Company and is the chief reason Jack's with them, his poker-faced obfuscation is no big surprise. Nor is the fact that Uncle Charlie can reach Jack when no one else can. Not even a wife. Or an almost ex-wife. Apparently, once a Company operative, always a Company operative. They must have some kind of secret code.

I don't even want to know. Or maybe I *do* want to know, and that's part of the problem. Once again, where Jack's concerned, I'm sitting squarely in the middle of ambiguity.

Uncle Charlie suggests everybody meet in an hour at the Turquesa. Apparently, he sensed my growing agitation, and thank goodness he didn't say the NoMoHeHaHo, which I couldn't find again, even if I'd dropped breadcrumbs. The Turquesa is poolside and has a huge breakfast buffet until eleven o'clock.

Everybody leaves my room except Uncle Charlie. Not a good sign. Something else is on his mind. As the level head in the Valentine bunch, I'm usually the one he confides in.

"You think Lovie is tied in with the bones my dog found?"

"I don't have enough information to make that call, but, yes, I do. I don't believe in coincidence."

"Neither do I." Just the opposite. I'm always looking for signs and wonders to help me steer my leaky boat through life's choppy waters without wrecking on a reef or capsizing and being eaten by sharks. "Do you think Fayrene's conversation with Lulu Farkle is tied into Lovie's disappearance? Alvin Farkle was crazy about her."

"But surely not crazy enough to kidnap her. Let's wait till Jack gets here before we make that call. He'll have more information."

"How?"

"You know I can't tell you that, dear heart. You must trust me. And him." Uncle Charlie hugs me and kisses my forehead. "Don't worry. We're going to find Lovie and Elvis. I'll see you downstairs in a bit."

After he leaves, I head straight to the shower. I'd love to take a long soak, but knowing Jack, he'll come barging in here any minute. Never mind that everybody else is waiting for him downstairs.

I don't recommend bathing while glancing over your shoulder. By the time I finish, there's a kink in my neck that I'm sure is going to take a big application of Biofreeze to get out and maybe even a heating pad.

I grab a pair of jeans and a white tee shirt, then slide my feet into a pair of Keds. These last few months—plus a few broken heels on some of my favorite shoes—have taught me that sleuthing and glamour don't mix.

Thank goodness, my hair is the good kind that requires nothing except a shake of my head and a quick run-through with the brush. A definite plus for an enterprising woman who makes a living steering others toward beauty.

Also a plus if you're trying to hurry out of your hotel bedroom before your over-the-top sexy almost-ex waylays you.

I find my way poolside with only one unplanned detour—to the "monumental" breakfast room where a group of undertakers wearing nametags with every state from Florida to Maine are hogging the doughnuts. One of them says, "It's about time you got here, Sylvia." Then he pinches me. Hard.

I'm happy to tell him I'm not Sylvia. As I leave, I jab a sharp elbow into my pincher's gut, then put a bunch of magnolias and molasses into my drawl as I apologize for being so clumsy. Whoever Sylvia is, she could take lessons from me.

Retracing my steps and heading in the right direction—I hope—I rub my hip. The pinch is sure to leave a bruise. Even more reason to keep out of Jack's reach. He has a list of faults a mile long, but he's the world's best protector. If he saw that bruise, he'd go looking for trouble.

By the time I get poolside, everybody else is there, including Jack. Spotting the back of his head—and all that dark, always-mussed hair—I wait till I can get my breathing back to normal before I join them.

Unfortunately, the only empty chair is beside him. Mama's machinations, no doubt. Or Jack's. When it comes to sneaky tactics, those two have cornered the market.

I slip into my chair. Without even looking at me, Jack puts his hand on my knee and says, "Cal," then continues telling the rest of the gang that he is heading to Tulum because he has reason to believe Lovie's being held somewhere near there.

"Then you think she's alive?" Rocky asks.

"If this is a kidnapping, and I believe it is, I always go into the search with the assumption the victim is alive."

The victim. I'm glad Jack's hand is still on my knee. I'd like to hide underneath it. I'd like to wrap myself in him and go to sleep and not wake up until Lovie prances in saying, *Get up lazybones, let's eat chocolate, let's party, let's get wicked.*

"We can use my men for the search." Rocky whips out his cell phone. "I'll call Seth and get him started."

"Wait." Jack lifts his hand from my knee. But only briefly, thank goodness. "The last thing we want is to have everybody thrashing through the jungle spooking the kidnapper."

"Why?" Fayrene pipes up. "I'd think a spoofed hijacker would hightail it."

"Jack knows what he's doing." Mama is getting hot under the collar, Rocky looks ill, and Jack bites back a chuckle. Only Uncle Charlie remains unflappable.

"Jack and I will go back to Tulum with Rocky. Callie, you can stay here to hold down the fort with Ruby Nell and Fayrene."

"Charlie Valentine," Mama says, "since when do you think I'm going to let you go off looking for my niece without me?"

"If Ruby Nell is going, so am I. After all, I'm the one who found out about the gentleman with Lovie on the ferry," says Fayrene.

"Fayrene, he was no gentleman," I say. "Besides, my dog is missing, too. He needs me."

"Elvis?" Jack's black-eyed stare makes me squirm. For more reasons than I'm fixing to talk about. "Why didn't you tell me you'd lost my dog?"

"He's not yours. If you care to remember, you're the one who left."

"All right, dear hearts. We'll all go to Tulum."

Jack stands up. "That's probably best. That way I can keep an eye on everybody."

He's looking straight at me when he says that. I don't know whether to slap him or kiss him.

As it turns out, I don't get to do either. Jack, Rocky, and Uncle Charlie hurry off to interview anybody on the island who might have seen Lovie and Elvis, leaving me to keep Mama and Fayrene out of trouble.

Famous last words.

Chapter 7

Folly, False Clues, and Farkles

As soon as the men are out of sight, Mama and Fayrene make a mad dash to the pier for some last minute shopping—interpret that, *tequila purchases*. I'm not opposed to another chance to shop for shoes. Suffice it to say, they don't have to hog-tie me and drag me along.

One hour, six bottles of tequila, and two new pairs of shoes later, we head back to the hotel where Fayrene calls home to give Jarvetis a blow-by-blow report on Lovie's *hijacking*.

After she hangs up, Fayrene says, "I told Jarvetis to call Bobby."

"Good idea," Mama says.

Those two believe Uncle Charlie's assistant is a true clairvoyant, but I've never seen evidence. I keep my mouth shut, though. If believing in Bobby Huckabee's psychic eye makes them feel better, who am I to burst their bubble? I pride myself on being the kind of woman you come to for comfort. Listen, this world's hard enough as it is without adding a bunch of pessimism to the mix.

"There's no use hanging around here waiting for the men to do all the detective work," I say. "Why don't I try to find Alvin Farkle while you two try to find Lulu and see just what she knows?"

"I've already told you." Fayrene is miffed, which is just what I need. On top of everything else.

"You did a good job, too, Fayrene, but it never hurts to dig a little deeper."

"Good idea, Cal. Come on, Fayrene. We'll separate and see if we can track her down."

"That won't be too hard, Mama. Everywhere the Arkansas folks go, the decibel level rises."

Mama sets off in the direction of the lobby, and Fayrene heads toward the pool. I guess I ought to be worried about letting Mama and Fayrene out of my sight, but I'm more worried about Lovie and Elvis. Who would want to kidnap them?

I decide to start my search on the beach. After all, that's where Lovie was last before she vanished. Besides, it's a gorgeous day, the view is spectacular, and any tourist in his right mind is going to be outdoors. Especially Alvin Farkle. If I remember correctly, his biggest worry about being an undertaker was losing his tan and looking as pale as his poor, unfortunate clients. Lovie said he spent more time in the tanning bed than I spend at shoe sales.

The beach is dotted with tourists sitting in beach chairs underneath the shade of umbrellas. I hardly give these a second glace. I'm looking for a very big beach towel with a well-oiled, hairy body. Not that I ever saw Alvin Farkle in the nude.

Thank goodness, Lovie kisses and tells. When she had her fling with Farkle, I learned more about him than I ever wanted to know. According to Lovie, he has as much body hair as an ape and his legs are so long he could wrap them completely around her (which makes them considerable, believe me). She gave me a blow-by-blow description of his other charms, too, but I'm too much of a lady to repeat what she said.

It doesn't take me long to spot Farkle, slick with suntan oil and spread out on a tropical-themed towel. Lovie was right. He's so hairy it's hard to find the turquoise toucans on his towel. I try, though. I can't look at him without blushing.

If I ever find Lovie alive, I'm going to kill her.

"Fancy seeing you here," I say. As interrogations go, it's lame, but it's a start.

He pushes his sunglasses to the top of his bald head. I'll bet he wishes he could redistribute some of that chest hair. I'd advise him about hair implants, but I don't think he'd appreciate it.

"Callie Jones?" He leaps off the towel and grabs me. It feels like being hugged by a gorilla. Holy cow! I'm glad Lovie has finally found her prince and quit trying to transform all these frogs. "Is Lovie with you?"

Is he sincere or is he trying to throw me off by hiding the fact that he knows where she is?

"Yes. She's around here somewhere."

"Great. Tell her I'd love to get together and talk about old times."

He sounds sincere, but he could merely be a very good liar. I decide to dig a little deeper.

"Lovie was at the beach yesterday. I'm surprised you didn't see her."

"I didn't come to the beach yesterday." Alvin shoves his sunglasses back into place. "My sister's never been to Cozumel, so the whole Arkansas group toured the island. We didn't even check into the hotel till late."

Is he talking so much because he's just told a lie or is he merely chatty? Lovie never mentioned his conversational skills, so I wouldn't know.

I try for puzzled innocence. "I saw Lulu at breakfast this morning." I'm not above lying if it's for a worthy cause. And I sincerely hope Lulu is his sister. Lovie never mentioned her. "I thought she said she had taken the ferry to Tulum yesterday."

"The island. Tulum. What difference does it make? If you want to book a tour, go see the hotel tour director."

Farkle flops onto his towel, turning his back, which is just as hairy as his front. I hate to be the one to disillusion him, but his tan does nothing to camouflage all that ugly black body hair. I'd recommend a hot wax treatment, but I don't intend to stand here in the middle of a foreign beach consorting with a possible kidnapper.

Without even saying goodbye, I jerk my cell phone out of my pocket and hurry back to the hotel.

"Mama, I've found Farkle. Where are you?"

"At the pool. We've found Lulu. Hurry."

Mama hangs up before I can ask her why. Her cryptic message chills me. Knowing Mama, something disastrous is afoot.

I take off running. Thank goodness for long legs and discipline and regular runs in my neighborhood. I'm not even winded when I reach poolside.

It doesn't take long to find out why Mama wanted me to hurry. She and Fayrene are chasing a skinny woman with sagging knees and crows' feet, yelling at the top of their lungs. *Wait, whoa, stop, slow down.*

If they'd spread out, they could flank her. They're so busy huffing and puffing, they haven't even seen me.

I set out in the opposite direction, hoping to hem Lulu Farkle in.

The woman needs some fashion advice. She's wearing a yellow bikini that washes out her complexion and does nothing for her figure. Plus, she has too much hair to be wearing a blunt bob. If I didn't intend to shake the truth out of her, I'd invite her to my room and cut some cute layers that followed her natural curl.

All that bushy black hair is a dead giveaway. She'd bound to be Lulu Farkle.

And I'm closing in. Victory is within sight when Lulu notices me and streaks toward the pool.

"Wait!" Fayrene yells. "We just want to integrate you."

"Are you broads crazy? Leave me alone."

Lulu jackknifes into the pool with hardly a ripple, then races toward the other side in a crawl worthy of Olympic contenders.

I'm almost close enough to plunge in after her, but Fayrene beats me to it. Her leap into the water sends a tsunami wave over a couple sunbathing on the rim. Saying words they must have learned from Lovie, they grab their soaking beach towels and storm off threatening to call the management.

Finally I'm close enough to dive in, and I'm proud to say I slice the water. Listen, I grew up on a farm with my very own lake. It was available any time I took a notion to swim and could convince the bullfrogs to get out of my way.

Unfortunately, Lulu must have grown up swimming, too. She's so far ahead of me, it's going to take every bit of skill I have to catch her.

"Quick, Mama. Intercept her on the other side." Just in case. Listen, I haven't been in the lake on the farm since Jack left. And I don't even want to talk about what we were doing. I'll say this much: not swimming.

Mama hasn't budged. What's wrong with her? All of a sudden, she yells, "Fayrene!"

Holy cow! Where is Fayrene? She went in but I never saw her come back up.

About that time, her head surfaces briefly, then goes back under.

Good grief. She's drowning. I alter course and head toward the green blob now rapidly sinking to the bottom.

Out of the corner of my eye, I spot Lulu clambering out of the pool and streaking off. If I ever get Fayrene off the bottom, I'm going to throttle her.

Fortunately, I have some help—a young man with enough muscles for the job. Together we get Fayrene onto the concrete apron. She sputters, sits up, and goes into complete Fayrene mode.

"I thought you were going to have to give me artificial perspiration."

"What did you mean, jumping into that water? You can't swim a lick." Mama helps Fayrene up and leads her toward the hotel to change clothes.

"I wanted to comprehend the criminal."

The man who helped rescue Fayrene looks a little startled, but he doesn't ask questions. I do, though. It turns out he's an undertaker from Dallas, Texas, who put himself through school working as a lifeguard.

I thank him, then hurry into the hotel for my own change of clothes. I sincerely hope Jack doesn't hear of this little episode. He'd have me on the next plane to Mooreville in less time than it takes me to shop a shoe sale.

Inside, I stop by Fayrene's room to check on her and Mama. Fayrene is on her cell phone telling Jarvetis about her "near death" experience. Mama is sitting by the window puffing on a cigarette without her movie star holder. She must really be upset.

I sit beside her, never mind that the smoke will pollute my lungs and do no-telling-what to my unused eggs.

"Flitter, I could wring her neck, jumping in the pool like that." Mama glares at Fayrene, who glares right back. "We might have found out something useful if she'd waited for you."

"I don't know, Mama. I didn't get much out of Alvin except to find out he lied about where he was yesterday."

"You think Alvin and Lulu are hiding something?"

"Maybe. But why kidnap Lovie? It's not as if she lied to him about her feelings or intentionally broke his heart."

"Maybe it wasn't his heart she broke; it was his ego."

"Or maybe he has it in for her over something we don't even know about."

Mama stubs out her cigarette. "We'll keep digging."

"Not today. We've got a ferry to catch."

Fortunately, it's getting dark by the time we board the ferry. I know Jack is already on here somewhere, but it's easy for me to lose myself in the crowd. I don't want to have to lie to him about our afternoon sleuthing fiasco. I want some time alone so I won't have to think about anything except finding my cousin and my dog.

Contrary to the ownership claims of Jack Jones.

Elvis' Opinion #5 on Tight Ropes, Jack's Socks, and Revenge

About the time that sleazy low-down skunk who kidnapped Lovie is vanishing into the jungle, I imagine Rocky is moaning, "Bring my baby back." Never fear. Elvis is on the job and taking care of business.

As soon as the coast is clear, I stroll into the shack, announcing my presence with a platinum-worthy rendition of "You Better Run." Then I prance over to the low-slung bunk and nuzzle Lovie's hand.

"Elvis? Is that you?"

Who does she think it is? Michael Jackson? Listen, they keep you longer than that before they let you come back down here in a dog suit—or any other kind of suit—and start messing around in the lives of humans.

Humans are fragile creatures. You have to know how to handle them before they turn you loose on terra firma with the kind of power I have.

Of course, to give Lovie credit, she's wearing a blindfold.

In case she might possibly mistake me for a jungle stray that wandered in, I do a little "Long Tall Sally." That snaps Lovie out of the doldrums and back into her sassy self.

She struggles halfway upright and swings her bound legs over the edge of the cot. "See if you can't gnaw these ropes off, Elvis. If I had my baseball bat, I'd beat the living tar out of the devil who did this."

Now she's talking. I sink my teeth into the ropes at her ankles and start gnawing. In case you're thinking this is easy for a dog with my teeth and talent, think again. I don't know where this hemp has been before it ended up wrapped around Lovie's legs. But trust me, it smells like Jack's old socks after they've been tossed behind the dirty clothes hamper and forgotten so long you could find a cure for disease growing among the folds.

One of the many reasons he ought to take Callie for a stroll around the Mooreville Truck Stop like I did my cute Frenchie. With that kind of romantic ambience, he could sweet-talk her into coming back to him. When he was living with Callie, every one of his socks smelled like Bounce dryer sheets.

Not that clean socks ought to be the main reason he makes up with my human mom. All I'm saying is hygiene matters. And Callie improves Jack's exponentially.

I lift my head from the ropes to keep from being asphyxiated.

"Hurry, Elvis. He might come back any minute."

Who does she think I am? Houdini? It's going to take me more than a few minutes to overcome the smell enough to set her free and keep down my last snack of Pup-Peroni.

Speaking of which, I haven't had a bite to eat in so long, that stupid monkey outside is starting to look tasty.

"Once we get out of here, I know you can track my kidnapper, can't you, Elvis?"

You bet your "Fame and Fortune." When I had women around the world throwing their panties at me and fainting at my feet, I had a cadre of people to find anything I wanted. I guess that's why I got sent back as a basset. With this famous nose, I don't have to rely on anybody else. I can sniff out everything from a hot-to-trot French poodle to a fresh shipment of pickled pigs' lips over at Gas, Grits, and Guts.

Lovie tries to work her feet loose, but the ropes are still holding tight.

"That's okay, Elvis. We'll get free. And when we do, that sorry piece of trash is going to wish he'd never messed with Lovie Valentine and Elvis."

There's a loud racket outside the door and we freeze.

"Quick, Elvis. Hide."

With Lovie sprawled on the cot, it's sagging so low I couldn't get underneath if I gave up Pup-Peroni for two years, and there's nowhere else in this room to hide. "Where Could I Go But to the Lord?" A frightening prospect. What if I got sent back as a cat?

Lovie and I hold our breaths, waiting for what happens next.

With an unholy screech, that dratted monkey jumps into the room, scaring me out of one of my incarnations.

I'm all set to show the jungle animal some

Mississippi muscle when he cocks his silly little head and stares at me like he knows me.

Of course, everybody knows the King.

"Is that a monkey, Elvis?" I whack my tail against Lovie's leg, a definitive yes. "He's got fingers. See if you can coax him over here to work on these ropes. You can talk animal talk, can't you?"

I can talk anybody's talk. Doesn't Lovie know? Music is the universal language.

I hum a few bars of "I'm Counting on You," and bless'a my soul if the little primate doesn't take a step toward us.

Who knows? Maybe he's the reincarnation of my pet monkey, Scatter, from my other life in Graceland.

Even better, maybe he's Abraham Lincoln, come to emancipate us.

Chapter 8

Ghastly Visions, Lost Tombs, and Grisly Discoveries

By the time we get to Tulum, it's too dark to traipse into the jungle and conduct a search. Still, I can hardly bear the thought of Lovie being out there somewhere. It's like having part of myself missing. That's how close we are.

And poor Elvis. Though he likes to pretend

he's up to every challenge, I picture my little Mississippi basset hound trying to cope with the Yucatan jungle.

Obviously, everybody in the Valentine party feels the same sense of loss and foreboding. As we trudge into the complex, I've never heard this group so quiet. Especially Mama and Fayrene. I haven't heard a single wisecrack from Mama nor any malapropisms from Fayrene.

With the dense jungles of Quintana Roo behind them, the ruins of Tulum look forbidding in the dark. Forget romance under a Mayan moon. I'll be glad to get inside the little guest cottage and pull the sheet over my head.

"We'll find them, Cal." Jack looms up suddenly beside me.

I'd be telling a lie if I said I wasn't glad to see him. It's like being watched over by some powerful Mayan deity.

Up ahead, Uncle Charlie comes to a halt. "Let's stow our bags, then meet on the steps of El Castillo in twenty minutes."

El Castillo is the major structure of Tulum, a small temple perched on the edge of the cliff overlooking the Caribbean. It's easy to find because it's the focal point of the ancient Mayan ruins.

As we enter the cottage, Mama and Fayrene head to their room and Uncle Charlie goes to his. Jack plucks my suitcase from my hand.

"I'll take care of this for you."

"I don't want you taking care of anything that belongs to me, Jack Jones."

I try to grab my bag from him, which is the equivalent of a wren trying to steal a breadcrumb from a crafty cat.

All I can do is follow along behind while Jack stalks through the cottage like he owns it. A modest stucco building, the four cubicles we call bedrooms are arranged along a narrow hallway. Two of the doors are already shut, and I can hear the steady drone of voices in Mama and Fayrene's room.

In the room across the hall, I hear Uncle Charlie moving around. Beyond is the tiny bathroom, then two other guest rooms. Mine and Jack's. Too close for comfort.

I don't have time to think about that now.

"Here we are." I stop in front of the room I occupied only yesterday.

Jack sets my suitcase inside the door and then scorches my skin with the most predatory look outside the jungle.

"Don't you even think about parking yourself in here, Jack. We're getting a divorce."

He doesn't say anything for such a long time I can feel my unused eggs dying. Finally he says, "You'll get the divorce, Cal. As soon as we're stateside again."

"Is that a promise?"

He's already halfway out the door. I'm certain he heard me, but I'm equally certain he's finished with the subject. Men are like that. They can shove a painful subject aside and then go about their business as if nothing happened.

Thank goodness I don't have time to dwell on the demise of my marriage. That combined with the kidnapping of Lovie and Elvis is almost more than I can bear to think about. I change into a cute pair of pink Steve Madden moccasins, throw on a pink sweater against the night breeze, then set out toward the central temple.

Flashlight beams puncture the darkness up ahead, and voices float toward me.

"I can't believe we beat Charlie here."

"I don't know why not, Ruby Nell. You were in such a hurry, you didn't even give me time to unpack my hand-crocheted African."

I'm glad poor Rocky isn't around to hear. He's already torn all to pieces over Lovie's disappearance. Fayrene's shocking malapropism could be his undoing.

The beams of light bobble as Fayrene and Mama circle behind the temple. There's a full moon out tonight. I guess they've decided to take a look at the Caribbean in the moonlight.

Lovie and Elvis could be somewhere out there in the dark. I pick my way to the edge of the jungle, cup my hands around my mouth, and call my dog. Dogs can pick up sounds humans can't possibly hear. If Elvis is out there somewhere, maybe the sound of my voice will guide him back.

I call him again, listen to the echoing silence of the jungle, then make my way back to the temple where I sit on the front steps to wait for the men. I need to come up with a plan. Usually this is easy for me. I'm a logical person. When Lovie and I were chasing killers in the Bubbles Caper and the Memphis murders, I was always the one to devise a viable plan.

Since Lovie was last seen on the ferry heading toward Tulum, I'm hoping Elvis is with her. The surrounding jungle is the logical place to start looking. I can hardly wait for daylight so we can get started.

And don't think for a minute I'm going to let Jack and Uncle Charlie leave me behind. Nothing's going to stop me. Not even jungle snakes.

High-pitched screams pierce the night.

"Mama!" I bolt up, race around El Castillo, and almost collide with them. "What in the world is wrong?"

"Ghosts." Mama points toward the sea. "They're throwing human sacrifices off the cliffs."

"Holy cow! You're hysterical."

"She's telling the truth." Fayrene is so out of breath, she's panting. "The haints tried to grab me. If I weren't so swift on my feet, I'd be their latest victim and Ruby Nell would be delivering my urology."

Maybe they've let our recent bout in Memphis with the Peabody killer go to their heads, or maybe they really did see something. In any event, I can't afford to stand around and do nothing. Lovie's gone and Mama might be next.

"Stay put." As I race in the direction Mama pointed, I hear pounding footsteps heading toward El Castillo. The men, I hope.

Pouring on a burst of speed, I round the building and almost lose my footing. Even in the moonlight, it's hard to see the rocks underfoot.

Suddenly an unholy howl sends chills over me. It's coming from my right. Jerking around I see a wisp of white disappearing over the wall and into the lethal-looking jungle growth.

"Stop!" I sprint after the glob of white.

Listen, just because I occasionally burn white candles and chant under the moon doesn't mean I believe in the moaning, groaning brand of ghost. I prefer to think of myself as open-minded and moderately mystical.

Putting on an extra burst of speed, I'm gaining on the so-called spirit when another appears out of left field and knocks me flat. No ghost I ever heard of is that solid.

Jack rounds the temple and scoops me off the ground. "Cal, are you okay?" I nod and he tells me, "Stay here." Then he's off in pursuit of the ghostly intruders.

Rocky lopes by and heads after him. They leap over the wall and vanish into the jungle. I'm torn between remaining there and trying to see or hear something that will give me a clue about the ghost chase, or hurrying back to check on Mama and Fayrene.

Suddenly a male voice yells, "They went that way," and El Castillo becomes chaos. Men appear out of nowhere, running in all directions, screaming to each other in languages I don't recognize. Well, Spanish, I can make out, but the others stump me. Apparently the ghostly visitors have spooked Rocky's entire archeological crew.

"Come, dear heart. Jack can handle it." Uncle Charlie is suddenly beside me, leading me back to Mama and Fayrene.

I expected to find them huddled together taking courage from each other. They're in a huddle, all right, but not the scared kind.

"I say we take the ferry to Cozumel tomorrow, bring back some floodlights, and flush those cowards out of their sheets," Mama says.

"I'm with you, Ruby Nell." Fayrene's face is no longer the color of her sweater. "If we don't do something fast, those haints are going to have their testicles all over the place."

Well, goodness gracious. *Tentacles,* I hope.

Obviously, Uncle Charlie managed to do the

impossible—talk them out of abject terror and into hard-core revenge in two seconds flat.

Men are still zipping past us with no apparent destination in mind. Occasionally, I hear bits and pieces of English—*ghosts, evil spirits, and grisly sacrifices.*

The moon vanishes behind a cloud, leaving us in pitch darkness, and I sense rather than see someone else approaching. If I were Elvis, my hackles would be up.

"Rocky's back from ghost chasing." The voice is male and gravely, one I don't recognize. "He's gone to calm down the men, but he said we should get away from this cliff and back to the main cottage."

"That's a good idea," Uncle Charlie says. "Thanks, Archie."

This must be Archie Morgan, Rocky's caretaker, if I remember correctly. The moon is still hiding, and I can't see much in the dark except that he's about three inches shorter than me.

"What about Jack?" My question is instinctive, and reveals more of myself than I want anybody to know, particularly Mama. I can feel her *I told you he's the one for you* look.

"He's still out there," Archie says.

Uncle Charlie puts his arm around me. "Don't worry, Callie. Jack's the best."

"He most certainly is." Mama has no idea that

she and Uncle Charlie are talking about two different things—Company undercover agent versus lover/husband.

All of us head toward the main cottage.

It's slightly larger than ours. For one thing, it has a living room, if you can call it that—six straight-backed chairs, a huge desk strewn with maps and Mayan artifacts, and one lumpy-looking brown couch (genuine Naugahyde, as Mama would say). The couch looks like it's not even conducive to sitting, let alone cuddling.

Two doors are open off the living room. Through one I see Rocky's hat on the bedpost and a dressing table that still holds Lovie's silver-handled brush. The sight of the brush almost makes me cry.

I quickly glance away through the other door. It leads to a short hallway with a small dining room (in case of bad weather, I guess) beyond. A serving bar connects the dining room to the kitchen, which is barely visible. I know from endless phone conversations with Lovie that there's a small room beyond the kitchen where Juanita and Rosita sleep. She always hated that they were so close by.

This place could use a woman's touch. No wonder Lovie's having such a hard time getting Rocky to discover her national treasure. When we find her, the first thing I'm going to do is whack the kidnapper senseless with my Jimmy

Choo stilettos. Then I'm going to help her spiffy up this place with candles and a few pretty Mayan textiles.

Mama and Fayrene sit down and proceed to take up the whole couch, so I sit on one of the uncomfortable straight-backed chairs. Uncle Charlie remains standing and so does Archie Morgan.

This man gives me the creeps. I don't know why. He's perfectly ordinary looking—thin gray hair, crooked nose, faded blue eyes, leathery skin that shows he has spent the last thirty-five years in the sun.

Even Fayrene seems uncomfortable around him. If Lovie were here we'd discuss why. Then she'd probably pick the lock of the caretaker's cottage, a little trick she learned from her brief fling with the hapless Slick Fingers Johnson, who is now doing time.

She wanted to teach me, but I asked her why she thought I'd ever need such a skill. Now I'm kicking myself for being so shortsighted.

And I'm missing my cousin the way you'd miss a leg or an arm. Why did I leave her on that beach in her condition? If I ever get her back, I'll never be careless with my best friend again.

As soon as we're all seated, Uncle Charlie takes charge, which always makes me feel better. I was a child when Daddy died, and in every major crisis of my life, I've turned to my uncle.

Well, Mama, too, but while Uncle Charlie's support is solid and his advice reasonable, she tends more toward the Lovie kind of comfort—chocolate and hugs and warm sweaters.

"There's no such thing as coincidence," Uncle Charlie says, and I echo, "Amen." Archie Morgan looks at me like I've lost my last marble, but Mama and Fayrene are right at home with my "front pew of the country Baptist Church" response.

"Ruby Nell, tell us exactly what you saw on the cliff tonight."

"Somebody was out there moaning and carrying on and trying to make me think he was a ghost."

"Only one?" Uncle Charlie asks.

Mama nods *yes,* but I tell him about my encounter with the second ghost. "He knocked me down. Which confirms my suspicions that the ghost was as alive as I am."

"Not exactly, Miss Ruby Nell." Archie Morgan shuffles to the center of the room. When he turns his insipid smile on Mama, I get the urge to knock it off his face. "Begging your pardon, ma'am, but I've been on this cliff a long time, and I've seen things that would raise the hair on your head."

"Are you fixing to stand there and tell me I don't know what I saw?" Like Elvis, Mama is quick to get her hackles up. Old man Morgan doesn't take offense. I'd feel better if he did. Mama can make a conquest without even trying. I don't even want to think about having Sunday dinner with this creepy old man.

"You saw something, all right, Miss Ruby Nell, but I think it was the real deal." Archie Morgan turns to me. "Your dog's discovery of my dearly departed Lucille's bones confirms what I've suspected for a long time. There's a Mayan tribe somewhere in the jungle still practicing the ancient rites of human sacrifice."

"Lord help us." Fayrene leaps off the couch. "Those cannonballs are going to eat Lovie and Elvis."

"Flitter," Mama says. "If there are cannibals in the jungle, they'd have gone after you and me."

"Ruby Nell Valentine, have you gone insane?"

"Think about it, Fayrene. We're tough old birds. Their meal would last much longer if we were the main dish."

"Good grief, Mama." I know she's trying to lift our spirits, especially after what old man Morgan just said, but I'm in no mood for frivolity. "Uncle Charlie's trying to find a connection between Lovie's disappearance and our ghostly visitors."

"Mrs. Johnson got it right," Archie Morgan says. "The cannibals are grooming Miss Lovie for their next sacrifice."

"There is no record of cannibalistic tribes in the jungle. My daughter is not going to be anybody's sacrifice. At first light, we'll have search helicopters in the air," Uncle Charlie says.

"They won't find anything. The jungle's too thick for choppers." Archie Morgan turns to Uncle Charlie. "No harm meant, sir, but your daughter looks a lot like my poor dead wife." He glances at a framed photograph of Lovie on Rocky's desk. "A goddess. The Mayans have conjured up ghosts to chase us off so we won't interfere with their grisly rites."

I may have to slap that old man, but Uncle Charlie looks like he's about to beat me to the punch.

"That's enough of that kind of talk. Tomorrow, Jack will work with the Mexican authorities on the cold case as well as coordinating the search for Lovie. Meanwhile, I want our own search teams in the jungle. We'll leave at first light. We'll debunk the ghost theory, and we *will* find my daughter."

Uncle Charlie visibly collects himself before he looks directly at old man Morgan. "We'll need every available man."

"I don't know how many will be left after tonight's ghost scare," Archie Morgan says. "And Rocky's going to need some of them to find the lost tomb."

"What's a lost tomb compared to a lost treasure?" Mama jumps off the couch, grabs Fayrene's arm, and motions to me. "Come on, Callie."

"Ruby Nell, where are you going?"

"Charlie Valentine, since when did you think you could leave the women out of the search?" She prances by my chair and jerks me up. "We're going to solve this mystery, Mooreville style. And don't you even think about trying to stop us."

For once I agree with Mama. This is my dog and my cousin. I'm not fixing to be left behind. Listen, Lovie and I have come up with some sleuthing plans that are doozies. I'm up to anything Mama wants to do. I just hope it doesn't involve tequila and cannibals.

Elvis' Opinion #6 on Ghosts, Tarantulas, and Being a Tasty Dog

I reckon I'm going to have to "Patch It Up" with the jungle monkey. Instead of calling him silly, I'm going to have to call him my new best friend. Before I can do a little "Shake, Rattle and Roll," he's got Lovie untied.

She rips off her blindfold and comes off that cot in a "Fever."

"When I find that jackass who did this to me, there won't be anything left of him but a greasy spot."

You go girl. I start sniffing around the shack to catch his trail while she storms around looking for clues. She snatches up her purse, discovers the scoundrel has run off with her cell phone and her ID, then lets out a yell that can be heard clear to Mississippi.

Meanwhile, our liberator, the little primate I'm now calling Abraham Lincoln—Abe for short— sits on a perch in the rafters twisting his head from side to side, watching us like we're specimens from another planet.

I wonder what he's thinking. Contrary to what I told Lovie, the only language I have in common with him is the universal one—music. Now, there's something everybody understands and loves. How do you think I became a household name in my other life as the world's sexiest man in sequins? I didn't just sing the songs and swivel my hips. I touched the heart and soul of my fans. I trapped them in the laser beams of my blue eyes and transported them into a world where you could believe in "Love Me Tender" and "Promised Land," cut loose with "Hound Dog," and weep with "Peace in the Valley" and "Heartbreak Hotel."

Lovie storms around the shack one last time. It's empty except for the cot, a rickety chair, and the smelly ropes.

"If that fool thinks I'm going to stand around here and starve to death, he doesn't know Lovie Valentine." She snatches up her purse. "Come on, Elvis. Let's get out of this rathole."

I trot over and she pats my head. "You can

track your way out of the jungle, can't you?"

I howl a few bars of "Reconsider Baby," hoping she'll see that it's pitch-black out there and it would be foolhardy for two Mississippi treasures to go tromping through a Mexican jungle. But Lovie ignores my opinion.

When I was packing the house in Las Vegas and throwing sweat-drenched scarves to women swooning at my feet, I was a god and my opinion was gospel. These days I'm lucky if I can get that silly cocker spaniel Callie calls Hoyt (in honor of one of my drummers) to part with his ham bone.

But never let it be said that Elvis Valentine Jones is missing backbone. I trot into that twisted jungle like I'm Tarzan of the Apes fixing to wrestle an alligator.

And speaking of apes, that silly little monkey scampers off his perch and follows us, swinging from tree to tree. If envy were in my nature, I'd be green. I'd much rather be up in the trees than down here with the pythons and tarantulas and anything else with the ability to suck the life out of me in one bite.

It's dark and dangerous out here. Bobby Huckabee would be predicting death around every bush. The moon is no help. Every five minutes, it disappears into the clouds, leaving us to stumble through the jungle.

A root the size of Texas leaps up to waylay Lovie, and she goes down with a thud. Abe screeches like he's just witnessed the Second Coming while I scamper backward to keep from being crushed in the fall. If there were any creepy, crawly things under Lovie, they're now toast.

She says a word that will get her permanently banned from the Pearly Gates, then she struggles upward.

"Elvis, are you sure you know where you're going?"

I do a little "It's Impossible," hoping she'll backtrack to the safety of the shack. Listen, I may be a hound dog with a tracking nose, but even this famous nose is not made to uncover a nonexistent trail in the middle of a tangled jungle. I'm as lost as one of the Lost Tribes of Israel. (I know my biblical history. In my other life as a young boy from the wrong side of the tracks, I learned to sing in a country church, which, by the way, was recently moved lock, stock, and wooden pews to the grounds of my Tupelo birthplace.)

As for this jungle adventure, personally, I'd rather take my chances with the kidnapper than with the tarantula I've just spotted. He's bigger than my mismatched ears.

If this were an ordinary spider back home in Mooreville, I'd swat him with my handy tail. But this is a Yucatan jungle we're talking about. Although I'm pure hero from my talented lips down to my sexy hips, I don't hanker after rash actions that could make me end up a poisoned pooch.

Lovie stops to assess our chances of getting out of here alive (bleak), says another word straight from a truck-stop bathroom wall, and then sets off at a brisk pace that says she's a woman it won't do to mess with.

A lesser basset would have complained that his legs are too short, but the King is up to any challenge. I hum a few bars of my hit, "We're Gonna Move."

Take note, you canine judges. Any fool watching me trot would give me a "Best of Show" award instead of pointing out that my back leg is slightly crooked.

An unholy howl stops Lovie in her tracks and puts my hackles on full alert.

"What was that?" she whispers.

But the jungle is eerily quiet. Even with my laser ears, I can't tell where the sound was coming from.

When it starts up again, the sound is multiplied a thousand times and coming from every direction. Lovie is no faint heart and I have the courage of a lion, but we wrap ourselves around each other like we've just heard Gabriel's trumpet announce the Second Coming.

Listen, whoever is out there is "Playing for Keeps."

"You'd better stop right there," Lovie yells. "I've got a gun and I'll shoot."

I growl to show we mean business.

Unfortunately, her threat is idle and I'm unarmed.

The howling, screeching, and caterwauling get closer, and all we can do is wait to see what happens next. It sounds like an army out there. Fisticuffs are out of the question.

Maybe negotiations will work. I howl a little "Peace in the Valley," but judging by the thrashing and screaming that's getting closer every minute, the natives are in no mood for a truce. Lovie and I have jumped out of the kidnapper's hands and straight into the lap of the devil.

Chapter 9

Mooreville Gossip, Half-Baked Plans, and More Trouble than the Law Allows

I feel a bit guilty about leaving Uncle Charlie alone with old man Morgan, but I have no other choice. In the first place, there's no telling what kind of trouble Mama and Fayrene will get into if I don't ride shotgun. And in the second, I'm not going to sit still while my cousin and my dog are missing.

Sometimes I wish I'd been born with a smaller conscience and a bigger attitude. Like Lovie. And I mean that in the nicest way. Shoot, if I were the one missing, she'd already be out there stomping around in the jungle with her baseball bat. Regardless of what anybody told her to do.

Mama and I trot toward the guest cottage like we're in the Barnes Crossing Mall back home, on the hunt for bargains. Fayrene keeps looking over her shoulder as if she expects a "cannonball" to reach out and eat her on the spot.

Suddenly she yelps and points. "Something's out there."

"It's your imagination, Fayrene," Mama says, but she's wrong. I see a wisp of white disappearing around the corner of our guest cottage. Not a ghost, I'm certain, but something even worse. A real, live person out to do us harm.

"What we need is some of Lovie's Prohibition Punch." I lead the way into the cottage then head to the little kitchen nook where all three of us fill generous-size mugs with our Southern comfort of choice.

Fayrene looks at her watch. "I ought to call Jarvetis."

"Go ahead," Mama says. "I'll be back in ten minutes and we'll be ready to roll."

"Mama, where are you going?"

"Just to my room. There's something I have to get."

I don't even want to know. In the last two days, I've had enough drama to last me the rest of my life. Sinking onto a stool beside the tiny bar, I sip my punch while Fayrene calls home.

Hearing her talk to Jarvetis about ordering more pickled pigs' lips and exclaiming over the people who came all the way from Paris (Tennessee, not France) to see their disco ball dance trophy makes me homesick. But I've never been a good liar. If I call Champ, he's sure to sense something is wrong. Then he'd gently prod until I told him the whole nine yards, including our encounter with ghosts.

He'd hop on the next plane, and then I'd really be in a mess. Luke Champion and Jack Jones can't be in the same city without getting into a male show-off contest. I don't want to imagine what they'd do if they were in the same guest cottage.

Mama bustles back, puffing away on a cigarette stuck in a 1930s movie star holder. If she's trying to get my goat, she's succeeded. For years I've tried to get her to quit smoking, but I'm not going to say anything. She says smoking calms her nerves.

Shoot, if I thought tobacco could calm mine, I'd take up smoking Cuban cigars.

Mama pours the last of Lovie's Prohibition Punch, plops onto the stool beside me, and places her Mayan guide book on the bar.

"It says here that the goddess Chalchiutlicue is called She of the Jade-Green Skirts."

"My favorite color!" Trust Fayrene.

"Mama, what does that have to do with anything?"

"Hold your horses, Miss Priss, and I'll tell you." She deliberately takes her time with her next drag on the movie star holder. "Elvis found the bones of Lucille Morgan near the temple of the goddess Chalchiutlicue." Big, dramatic pause and another long, drawn-out drag of her cigarette. "The goddess was a glutton for sacrifices. Females only."

"Holy cow! That awful old man might have been onto something when he talked about sacrifices."

"Virgin sacrifices?" Fayrene wants to know.

"Lord, no. The guide book says they took the cream of the crop. My niece hasn't been a virgin since she hit puberty."

No need to ask how Mama knows. Like all mothers, she has eyes in the back of her head. I just hope my deprived eggs hold on long enough for me to find out if I can grow another set of eyes.

"Mama, you're scaring me. If the location of the bones is significant and Lovie's disappearance is linked to that of Lucille Morgan, then we have to work fast."

"Poor Lovie. Eaten alive." Fayrene starts crying. "I wonder if they used salt."

"For Pete's sake, Fayrene. My niece is too smart to be eaten alive, with or without salt. All we have to do is get out to the temple, tempt the goddess, and draw the kidnappers out of hiding."

"Mama, you've got to be kidding."

"Do you have a better plan, Callie?"

"Unfortunely, no." If she'll care to remember, my plans for questioning the Farkles didn't go well.

Mama squashes out her cigarette, swigs her last drop of Prohibition Punch, and says, "Then shake a leg."

"Where are we going?"

"To sacrifice ourselves to a goddess."

I don't know why I even asked. The crazy thing is that Mama could be right. If there is a connection between Lovie and Lucille Morgan, the kidnappers are more likely to be locals using Mayan mythology to cover their crimes than an ex-lover with a bruised ego and his fashion-disaster sister.

If anybody can tempt She of the Jade-Green Skirts, it's Mama. And she's already three strides ahead of me, strutting down the hallway, probably imagining herself as the cream of the crop.

Thirty minutes ago in the safety of the guest cottage, tempting a kidnapper/killer/ghost seemed like a pretty good idea. The plan even held water when Mama suggested we all put on some of Fayrene's green skirts and do a dance on the temple steps to draw the enemy toward the goddess who loves green.

But now, stumbling through the dark behind Mama and Fayrene, I'm wondering how I let myself be conned into such a half-baked plan. I don't know which is likely to happen first: Fayrene's big green skirt will fall off my skinny frame, killer ghosts will drag the three of us into the jungle to do no-telling-what-all, or Fayrene will run into a tree in her night-vision goggles.

Who else would pack night-vision goggles for a trip to an undertakers' convention? When I asked why, she said, "In case of immersions."

I think she meant emergencies, but unless our off-the-wall plan succeeds, every last one of us will be up to our necks in hot water.

Somewhere in the dark, something moans. Or *somebody*.

"Mama, did you hear that? Somebody's out there."

"Of course. Why do you think I suggested we all pack heat?"

"Mama, a brass lamp base is not heat."

"It's better than nothing. Besides, when we scream, Charlie will come running."

"You didn't mention anything about screaming."

"If I had, do you think Fayrene would have come?"

Up ahead, Fayrene looks like some kind of zombie in her night-vision goggles. She's marching forward stiff legged with her hands held out in front of her.

"How're you doing up there, Fayrene?" Mama yells.

"If a ghost is out here, I can spot him a mile." She plows in to the side of the temple, which she couldn't even spot three inches ahead. Or else the temple leaped out of the dark to waylay her. "It ought to be against the law to move buildings around."

I don't ask her how that happened. I'm afraid her explanation would make sense.

We assemble at the base of the temple, which looks imposing and mysterious, even a bit scary. What if old man Morgan is right? What if cannibals are lurking in the dark to sacrifice a female to the goddess of the Jade-Green Skirts? I wish I was wearing red.

Shoot, I wish I were in Mooreville with Elvis and Hoyt and the seven cats. I wish I had nothing more important on my mind than keeping Jack Jones from waylaying me in my own bed.

Mama tries to take charge. As usual.

"Okay. Callie, you and Fayrene climb to the top and start dancing."

"What are you going to do, Mama?"

"Stand guard with my brass lamp."

"You can't hit the side of a barn, Ruby Nell.

How do you think you're going to hit a ghost?"

"Shut up and dance, Fayrene. Leave the rough stuff to me."

"Mama, there's not going to be any rough stuff. If we actually do draw the kidnapper out of hiding, we're going to scream and run to get Uncle Charlie." I don't even mention cannibals for fear of spooking She of the Night-Vision Goggles.

"Who do you think raised you, Carolina Valentine Jones? Fairies?"

"Mama, I don't think child rearing prepares you to subdue a killer."

"Wait till you and Jack have kids."

"If you'll care to remember, we're getting a divorce."

"Ha."

"*Ha* is not a word."

This is getting us nowhere fast. We might as well be in Mooreville discussing hairdos and nail colors instead of in the Yucatan trying to solve a mystery.

"Okay, truce, Mama. Let's get this show on the road and smoke out the villain."

I just hope we only smoke out one. We might stand a chance, three against one. Or two and a half against one, if you count that Fayrene is still wearing her goggles and can't see a building, let alone a villain.

"Let's all make a circle and hold hands," Mama says.

Apparently she has changed her mind about standing guard. I guarantee the decision was entirely about her and had nothing to do with my arguments. Mama sets the lamp base down within easy reaching distance and grabs my hand.

"I'll summon the spirits." Fayrene joins hands with us and completes the circle. "I've been practicing."

"For what?" Mama wants to know.

"For when we finish the séance room at Gas, Grits, and Guts."

Fayrene starts chanting in a high-pitched, ethereal voice that would probably alert dogs for miles around. I'm not so sure about ghosts.

Still, she's creating a rhythm, and we all fall into it. I wonder if you can fool Mayan goddesses. From where I'm stomping and swirling, it looks more like we're circling the wagons than attracting She of the Jade-Green Skirts. Besides, the sight of Fayrene in her goggles is likely to scare spirits off. Plus, her weird wailing sounds like she's doing inventory at Gas, Grits, and Guts.

"Beanspeascorn, pea-nut but-ter. Mustardketsup, to-ma-to soup. Salt,pepper, cu-cum-bers."

I don't think Mama's aware we're dancing to the tune of a grocery list. She has a rapt look that means she's tuned out everything around her. Mama's good at that. She tunes out my opinion every time I have one. If I let that bother me, I would never have a single word to say about anything. And we all know that's not true.

A sliver of moon peeks from behind the clouds. I take that as a good sign. Listen, I know it doesn't take much to encourage me, but with the two I love best missing, I'm willing to grab ahold of the least little thing that gives me hope.

Okay, one of them is a dog, but that doesn't count. Elvis makes a better friend than some people I know.

"Keep going, girls." Always a good dancer, Mama's really into the rhythm. "Any minute now, we're going to rouse the goddess."

I hear a rustling sound coming from the direction of the jungle. We've roused something, all right, but I doubt it's a goddess. It sounds like something much more sinister.

I peer into the darkness, trying to catch a glimpse of white. Fayrene's sudden scream scares the moon back into hiding. Mama bumps into her, I bump into Mama, and we all tilt dangerously toward the left.

A big dark figure appears, braces Fayrene, and tilts us all upright again. She rips off her night-vision goggles and starts swinging.

"I'm a ghost hunter, and I'm deadless."

Mama reaches down to grab her brass lamp base and I go into a karate stance. I've never taken a minute of karate lessons, but I'm hoping our assailant won't know my only instruction in martial arts came from watching *The Karate Kid* with Lovie.

"Come any closer, and you can kiss your life goodbye." Mama sounds authentic. If I didn't know better, I'd think she made her living hunting down vicious criminals.

Out of the dark, somebody chuckles. I'd know that laugh anywhere, and it's no ghost.

"You can put the lamp down, Ruby Nell." The moon scuttles out from behind the cloud and Jack Jones materializes out of the shadows. I don't know whether to hug him or hit him with Fayrene's night-vision goggles.

I like to think I can take care of myself. But Jack rescues me with a regularity that would be depressing if I let myself dwell on the negative. Which I don't. I pride myself on being a positive person.

Jack leans against one of the temple's pillars. His pose looks casual, but I know him too well to be fooled.

"What are you three doing out here?"

Fayrene giggles. She always gets a bit giddy around my almost-ex. I would, too, if I were married to Jarvetis. And I mean that in the kindest way. Fayrene's husband is a nice man, but nobody would ever mistake him for a hunk. Especially one of Jack's proportions. Jarvetis looks kind of like a long, tall, skinny basset hound.

"We're tempting the goddess of the Jade-Green Skirts." Fayrene puts her goggles back on. I guess the better to view Jack's muscles.

"Any luck?" He's acting like a man carrying on a conversation around a Sunday dinner table instead of one who's been in the jungle chasing heaven only knows what.

"Not yet," Mama says. "But we're fully prepared."

"Good. I want you to stay that way." He unfolds himself and drapes an arm over Mama's shoulders. "Allow me to escort three beautiful ladies inside."

"Next time maybe we'll sacrifice a chicken," Mama says.

"Next time, call me. You never know when you're going to need a lethal weapon."

I don't miss the wicked look Jack gives me. His weapon is lethal, all right, but if I let myself start thinking about that right now, there's no telling where it would lead.

"By the way, Ruby Nell, I enjoyed the dance," he says to Mama. "When we get back home, you'll have to do a repeat performance."

I see through Jack Jones. While he makes small talk, he's herding us back to the safety of the guest cottage. The path is narrow, plus the moon has vanished again. Permanently, it seems. We head upward single file, first me, then Mama, Fayrene, and Jack.

There's a sound ahead of me, and I sense rather than see that we are not alone. I stop so suddenly, Mama and Fayrene bump into me.

"Stop right there. Identify yourself." Jack's command is a welcome reminder that we have an escort who is more than capable of defending us.

"Juanita, señor. I was taking clean sheets to the cottage."

At this time of night? Why doesn't Jack challenge her? Especially in light of events. If Mayan magic is being used in Lovie's kidnapping, then the Farkles—or whoever the culprit is—had to have some inside help, somebody close enough to Tulum to pull off the ghost stunts.

Maybe Juanita wasn't delivering clean sheets. Maybe she was grabbing some for her nightly rounds as the ghost of Tulum.

Jack lets her pass without a word. Still, I'd hate to be in her shoes. Silence from Jack Jones does not mean you're off the hook. About anything.

Once we're inside, Jack tells us to stay at the door, then he goes through every room in the cottage. I don't want to even imagine what he's looking for. Another missing person's bones? A body? Lovie's body? Fear feels like ice water in my veins.

"Where's Uncle Charlie?"

Suddenly Jack is back.

"Consulting Rocky. Don't worry. Everything's

okay." He slides his arm around me. I'm so grateful for the body heat, I don't protest.

"Good night, Jack." Mama stands on tiptoe and kisses his cheek.

" 'Night, Ruby Nell, Fayrene. Lock your doors and don't come back out till morning."

"That sounds omnibus."

"It is." He manages to interpret *ominous* from Fayrene's garbled English. After she and Mama are behind closed doors, he leads me down the hallway, which has suddenly become six hundred miles long.

I try a little small talk of my own.

"Did you find anything in the jungle?"

"No."

"Are you telling me the truth or just trying to protect me?"

Instead of answering, he pins me against my very own door.

"Cal, I want you to promise me the three of you won't go out again at night by yourselves."

"Give me one good reason I should listen to you."

"How about this? If you don't behave yourself, I'm going to be the one getting into your jade-green skirt."

He opens my door, scoops me up, deposits me on my bed, then stands there looking at me like I'm the sacrifice and he's the hungry god.

Callie no-is-my-middle-name, becomes Callie

who-can't-say-no. If Jack makes one move, I'm a goner.

Fortunately, he marches out and shuts the door. I listen to his footsteps as he goes back down the hall.

From now on, he's going to be watching every move Mama, Fayrene, and I make. If we want to locate Lovie before she becomes a sacrifice "with salt," as Fayrene says, we've got to keep our plans a deep, dark secret from Jack Jones.

Elvis' Opinion #7 on Dignity, Enemies, and Unsavory Stew

The enemy is closing in. With wild banshee howling, the thundering mob heads our way. In the dark, they sound like tens of thousands. Even if there are only two of them, Lovie and I are outnumbered.

"Run, Elvis!"

Like I need any encouragement. But where is there to run? The "Big Boss Man" is coming, and I don't see any "Bridge Over Troubled Water."

We streak off, running full tilt till an elephant-size tree rears up in our path.

"Don't worry, Elvis. We're making great progress."

I wonder if all those drinks with the tiny umbrellas impaired Lovie's ability to measure distance. My idea of great progress is more than three yards.

"Which way, Elvis?"

My preference would be up. I'd howl a little "Swing Down Sweet Chariot" but I don't think they send down heavenly escape buggies to rapture folks who've led the checkered lives Lovie and I like to brag about.

Suddenly we're surrounded and there's no way out. From the looks of those spears they're carrying, I'd say this is not the welcoming committee. The moon shows itself long enough for me to see that we're in the clutches of savages with the kind of painted-up faces you see when you leave off a good dream of chasing rabbits and end up having your worst nightmare.

In a last-ditch effort, Lovie turns on her famous charm.

"Listen, fellows, let's talk about this. I'm just a sweet little old lady out for a walk with Elvis. You know Elvis? 'Blue Suede Shoes'?"

Lovie launches into one of my biggest hits. She has a good alto voice, but she's picked the wrong song. She's the only one in this crowd wearing shoes.

Besides, I don't think these men are music lovers. Two bars into the song, they break ranks and grab us. Our new captors are each hardly bigger than a border collie. I could take them down in two minutes flat except for one thing:

they're carrying real spears. And I don't hanker to become known as the famous dog who got sliced into tasty bits in less time than it takes to howl "I'm Gonna Walk Dem Golden Stairs."

Lovie yells, "Stop it. You can't do that. We're U.S. citizens. Call the embassy. Call the White House."

Lovie's barking up the wrong tree. These savages probably don't even know what a house is, let alone the White House.

After they truss us up tighter than a Thanksgiving turkey, our captors launch into a heated discussion. Probably about our fate.

"What are you saying? What are you going to do with us? I demand answers. Tell them, Elvis."

Listen, I'm a musical genius, not a linguistics professor. How do I even know what they're saying?

Finally we set off again. Unfortunately, it's not golden stairs Lovie and I walk, but eighty-five thousand miles of jungle, and every treacherous mile of it out to do us in.

Unless we get skewered first by the tip of a lethal spear.

The indignity of it all. I'm glad Hoyt and Callie's seven silly cats aren't here to see me. Don't these savages know who they're dealing with? In 1970, I was a personal guest of President Richard Nixon. Listen, the capture of a famous dog like me could cause an international incident.

The minute I get free, I'm writing the current administration. I'm demanding apologies.

Of course, if these painted-up, raging maniacs are cannibals with a taste for a tasty dog, Lovie and I are going to end up in hot water. And I'm talking more than trouble. I'm talking stewpot.

Chapter 10

Secrets, Searches, and Diabolical Twists

At the crack of dawn, I'm jerked out of a fitful dream of ghosts by pounding on my door. Before I can even say, *Come on in,* Mama prances inside, plops onto my bed, and proceeds to make herself right at home.

She's wearing a blinding orange nightshirt featuring an embroidered gold crown on the front plus the slogan WHO DIED AND MADE YOU QUEEN? And she's still in her take-charge mood. Thank goodness she's not puffing on that ridiculous movie star cigarette holder, polluting my eggs with nicotine before they ever have a chance to get fertilized.

"I've consulted Bobby."

"Holy cow, Mama. Bobby's a nice guy, but he's a fake."

"His blue eye is psychic."

"If Bobby really has a psychic eye, I'd have called him, myself."

"He said we're surrounded by danger."

"He always says that. For goodness' sake, Mama. Lovie and Elvis are missing, and Rocky's up to his neck in Mexican authorities conducting a murder investigation."

"Flitter, what do they know? I've consulted my guide book. I think we were on the wrong track trying to appease She of the Jade-Green Skirts."

"Now you're talking some sense. I think Juanita is in on it. She could be in cahoots with that creepy old man Archie Morgan. Or maybe she is Alvin and Lulu Farkle's inside contact."

"She wouldn't say boo to a cat. And I'm not convinced Archie Morgan or the Farkles had a thing to do with the kidnapping."

"Mama, it's too early to rule anybody out. If the ghost sightings are connected, we know that at least two people are in on this. Maybe more. I saw at least two ghosts."

"Flitter, you didn't see any ghosts."

"Okay. People in bedsheets. And what was Juanita doing heading to our cottage so late last night?"

"Forget about the maid. The thing we've got to do is have a ceremony in the light of Venus so we can channel our inner animal."

So much for sense. Mama's outrageous new

plan makes me wonder if I was left on her doorstep by traveling gypsies.

How can I possibly share the same DNA as somebody so totally off the wall? Of course, there was the time I deliberately got into a hot air balloon with a suspected Elvis killer. And the time in Memphis when I nearly got arrested breaking and entering in a maid's uniform.

Okay. I'll admit it. I have more in common with Mama than first meets the eye. Still, channeling my inner animal is not high on my list of priorities.

"Mama, forget about inner animals. While the men search for Lovie and Elvis, we've got to find out more about old man Morgan and his wife."

"What could possibly be the connection between a thirty-year-old murder and Lovie's disappearance?"

"Are you defending that old man?" If she is, I've got bigger troubles than I ever imagined.

"I'm just talking sense, Carolina."

"There's no need to get huffy, Mama. You know we have to look at every possibility, and that means finding out what we can about Archie Morgan. We've also got to see what his connection is to Juanita and the Farkles. There's no such thing as coincidence."

"You sound like Charlie."

Mama tries for gruffness, but I'm beginning to

see through her. Underneath all that bluff and bluster is a woman who would die before she'd let harm come to those she loves. And that includes Uncle Charlie and Lovie as well as me.

I'm not like Uncle Charlie, though. While he will rely on common sense and his past experience with The Company, I'll rely on instinct and incense, signs and stars, and anything else that will lead me to Lovie and my silly, lovable, hip-swiveling, lip-curling dog. Well, anything except channeling my inner animal.

"As soon as Fayrene gets up and the men leave," I tell Mama, "we're going to sneak into the main cottage and do some serious snooping."

"Why there?"

I tick the reasons off on my fingers: "Rocky's files. His computer. He'll have records of everybody working in Tulum. Besides, the room shared by the maid and the cook are there. I want to find out what Juanita's up to."

A blood-curdling scream catapults me off the bed. I race toward the door, never mind that I'm barefoot and barely covered by a pair of retro pink pajamas the fashion magazines call *baby doll*. Mama is right behind me.

"We need a weapon."

She's right. As we pass my closet, I grab one of my Jimmy Choo stilettos off the floor. Mama grabs the other. Listen, we may look like silly women speeding to the rescue in our nightclothes wielding designer shoes, but I wouldn't want to be on the business end of a Jimmy Choo high heel. Why do you think they call these things stilettos?

The screams echo down the hall again. Coming from the bathroom, it sounds like. Judging by the pitch and volume, I'd say whoever is in there is either being hysterical or being salted for the stewpot.

Mama and I are speeding toward the bathroom when the door pops open and Fayrene flies out.

I grab her shoulders to keep her from running all the way to South America. The way she's flying, she could walk on water. "What's wrong?"

"Deadless snakes!"

Holy cow! If you think I'm going to get close enough to a snake to bop him over his tiny, lethal head with a Jimmy Choo stiletto, you're crazy.

Apparently, Mama feels the same way. She's already running toward the front door, screaming loud enough to be heard in Mooreville.

"Where?" I ask, but Fayrene stands there with her lips quivering. I give her a little shake. "Where are the snakes?"

"Bathtub." She jerks loose, then races after Mama, her green seersucker gown flapping behind her. Their combined screeching is enough to rouse every dead god and goddess in Tulum.

Now what? I've got to come up with a plan. It'll take those snakes about three seconds to decide there's nothing in the bathroom worth biting, and then they'll come slithering out of the tub looking for me. It takes me less than a second to decide Mama's plan is brilliant.

Besides, three screaming women are better than two. I'm not ashamed to admit I can screech with the best of them. Still clutching my Jimmy Choo heel, I speed down the hall after Mama and Fayrene.

And right into the arms of Jack Jones.

"Nice outfit." I could be tied to train tracks in the path of a speeding train, and he wouldn't let the opportunity for a suggestive remark pass. "You okay?" All I can do is nod. "Get out of the cottage, Cal. Go!"

He heads straight toward the bathroom. Obviously Mama and Fayrene have already told him about the snakes. What he's going to do, I don't know. I don't even want to know.

As I race out of the cottage I catch a glimpse of a man and a woman disappearing around the corner. From the back, I can't tell who the man is, but judging by the woman's hair—my area of total expertise—I'd swear the female is Rosita.

What's the cook doing so far away from the kitchen? Especially right at breakfast time.

Besides, if I'd laid bets on who was behind the snakes, I'd have said Juanita of the Clean Sheets.

I don't stop running till I'm in the courtyard behind the main cottage where Fayrene and Mama are recounting their tale of snake terror to Uncle Charlie. Both talking at the same time.

I pour myself a cup of coffee, then sink into a straight-backed chair at the table. But not before I've inspected it for deadly crawling creatures. The first sip fortifies me, and the second makes me feel almost human again.

Listening to Mama and Fayrene tell about our fright this morning, I wouldn't even recognize it as the event that scared them out of their wits and probably left my poor unused eggs so traumatized they'll never be fertile again. On the other hand, both of them thrive on drama. To hear them tell it, they would have waded into those snakes and wrung their mean little heads off to protect me.

I've never had a flair for drama, even as a child. In school plays I was always the kid picked to stand in the back row and be a cabbage. Plus, my eye twitches when I tell a lie.

"First the ghosts and now this." Mama pours herself some coffee and sits beside me. "Charlie, somebody's definitely trying to run us off."

"I think you're onto something, Mama."

Whatever Uncle Charlie thinks he's keeping to himself. Probably, he's thinking that if he confirms Mama's suspicions, he'll add to our stress. His MO is serve and protect.

Listen to me. If I'd said that out loud, I'd sound just like Lovie after she's watched too many film noir movies.

"Where's Rosita?" I try to make this question nonchalant. I don't want Mama and Fayrene any more riled than they already are.

Before anybody can answer, Rocky rushes into the courtyard hatless, disheveled, and frantic. Now what?

"Ghosts prowled Tulum all night and five of my men have run off." He grabs a doughnut, heads toward the table, sees us practically in our underwear, and does a quick shuffle backward. Ever the perfect gentleman, he even makes a half-turn so his back is to us.

Listen, I don't approve of our being out here practically naked any more than he does, but I'm not about to barge into a cottage full of snakes just so I can look presentable on the outskirts of a jungle.

"Jack's on it," Uncle Charlie tells Rocky. "He'll find out who's at the bottom of your problems, and I can guarantee it won't be ghosts."

"I appreciate that, Charlie, but I don't know how I'm going to carry on my archeological work while I oversee a murder investigation and search for Lovie."

Mama perks up and is all poised to put her two cents in, but I shake my head. Let the men do what they want. The women have a different plan.

"Don't worry about a thing, boss." Seth strolls into the courtyard. I didn't even hear him approach, which is not like me. "Archie can keep the remaining men on task while you and I search the jungle for Miss Lovie."

Seth proceeds to fill his plate, then plops down at the table ignoring our nightclothes. "Are you ladies having a good morning?"

"Fayrene found snakes in the bathroom this morning," Mama says.

"I'm about prostate with fear."

Poor Rocky chokes over Fayrene's miraculous body part, but Seth is unfazed.

"Around here, they're a minor nuisance."

Is he kidding or is he just trying to make light of a bad situation?

Suddenly the air sizzles with a different kind of energy. Jack is standing by the entrance to the courtyard. He might as well be a stick of dynamite. And not only where I'm concerned. Seth gets very quiet, and his shoulder muscles bunch up. I'd never noticed he had so many. Up close, he looks like a contestant for Mr. Atlas.

Jack strolls casually to the table, but there's nothing casual in the way his black eyes bore into me. Without a word about the snakes, he places a map on the table.

"I've laid out the search area in quadrants."

Overhead, helicopter blades beat the air, a sober reminder of Lovie's plight.

Seth rallies, then pops up to inspect the map. "Great idea, Jack. Rocky and I will take the north quadrant. You and Charlie start with the east."

Jack sizes Seth up with a look that turns the brash young man's face bright red. Then he nods to Uncle Charlie. What's going on here? More than Jack and Uncle Charlie will ever tell, I'm sure. Even under questioning.

I'm next on Jack's list of people he can undo with a single look. Sweat rolls down the sides of my face, and if I squeeze my Jimmy Choo shoe any harder, the heel's going to pop off.

"Cal, the cottage is safe now." He's clearly dismissing me. Mama and Fayrene, too, of course.

"What about the snakes?"

"Dispatched." Jack says this the same way he might tell me he sent his best friend for a three-day vacation to Vicksburg where you can get on a riverboat and gamble on the mighty Mississippi River. Legalizing gambling was another major lapse of judgment by certain politicians, might I add.

I could sit here and play games with Jack and wish I didn't have gambling practically in my back yard to tempt Mama, but I have other plans. Which I hope will remain undetected by my almost-ex. Plus, I want him in the jungle leading the search for Lovie and Elvis.

I stand up. "Mama, Fayrene, let's grab breakfast and take it to the Temple of the Frescoes so we can eat by the sea."

Thank goodness, Mama catches on and doesn't argue. Fayrene is another story.

"I thought we were going to help solve this mystery before there's another futility."

Poor Rocky. It's hard enough for him to get his mind around the fact that Lovie might be a fatality, much less a futility.

But what's up with Jack? Why is he not ordering me to stay put? At the breakfast buffet table, I load up a plate with doughnuts. Being around Jack always does that to me. All that energy I have to pour into restraint, I guess.

Balancing my plate and my coffee, I'm headed back toward the cottage with Fayrene and Mama when Jack says, "Cal, Archie Morgan will be keeping an eye on you ladies while we're gone. Let him know if you need anything."

"Good idea," Seth says.

He doesn't have a clue. When Jack Jones is this casual and offhand, you'd better be watching your back and digging for motive.

"Thanks, Jack." Mama smiles and waves at her almost-ex son-in-law.

The minute we're out of earshot, I say, "Mama, are you kidding me? That's his way of keeping tabs on us."

"I know."

"If you knew, why'd you say thanks?"

"Carolina, you catch more flies with honey than vinegar."

Maybe she's right. But in case she hasn't noticed, Jack is hardly a fly.

The guest cottage is just up ahead. I'm not as anxious to enter as I was to leave. Obviously Mama and Fayrene feel the same way. If the three of us slow down any more, you won't even know we're moving.

"I'm not going in that bathroom by myself," Fayrene says.

"What do you think best friends are for? If you need to go to the bathroom, just call Cal. She'll go with you."

This is one of those times I wish Mama would speak for herself. Still, I'd want somebody with me if I were reentering a room recently occupied by "deadless" snakes.

It takes us less than two minutes to change out of our nightclothes into shorts and tee shirts. Mama and Fayrene grab hats, I secure my hair against the heat in a hasty French twist, and we get the heck out of Dodge, as Lovie would say. Only she wouldn't say *heck*.

Since Jack will surely have Archie Morgan spying to see if we actually go to the Temple of the Frescoes, we head that way. Over doughnuts and coffee, we discuss how to sneak into the main cottage without detection.

"Disguises," Mama says. "This place will soon be crawling with tourists. All we have to do is disguise ourselves to look like them."

"Does that mean I have to wear something besides green?"

"Cheer up, Fayrene," I tell her. "We won't be wearing disguises."

"Flitter. I'd like to know why not?" Mama hates being wrong.

"Because Archie Morgan will be watching. He wouldn't let a tourist into the main cottage any more than he'd want us snooping around there."

"What are we going to do?" Mama asks.

"The two of you are going to create a diversion while I sneak in. Then you're going to hotfoot it back to your rooms. I'll meet you after I finish snooping."

"What kind of diversion?" Fayrene wants to know.

"I've got a plan." Mama perks up at being back in charge.

Even if it involves channeling her inner animal, I don't care. All I need is enough time to get on Rocky's computer to do some cyber-snooping, then search the room off the kitchen where Juanita and Rosita sleep.

Considering that we've already been through a kidnapping plus encounters with ghosts and snakes, the hard part's over.

What else can possibly go wrong?

Elvis' Opinion #8 on Foes, Big Macs, and Monkey Business

Well, bless'a my soul. Here we are in a primitive village so remote it's probably not even on the map.

The painted-up savages lead us to a little thatched hut and shove us inside. Lovie's gagged so she can't protest, and my paws are so scratched up, I'm grateful to be anywhere but traipsing through the jungle.

I'm so tired when I plop down on the mat, I don't know whether to growl "Release Me" or "Reconsider Baby." Lovie thrashes around to let me know she's as far from "Surrender" as you can get. If she thinks I'm going to drag myself over there and start gnawing ropes in front of restless natives carrying sharp-pointed spears, she's fried a few brain cells with her own Prohibition Punch.

Even that empty-headed monkey is not foolish enough to untie her ropes and stir up the natives. He followed us all the way through the jungle, and is now up a tree outside our hut chattering as if he had something to say.

He might as well keep his trap shut. I can't understand monkey talk any better than I can cannibal talk. Even my famous mismatched ears are no match for fools not speaking English.

Let me tell you, if I spoke that monkey's language, I'd tell him to get out there and scavenge up some food. The King never goes hungry. Back in my heyday as a worldwide icon with black sideburns, I could call down to Graceland's kitchen any time of the day or night and everybody would scurry to fix whatever I wanted. Usually a fried peanut butter and banana sandwich. Sometimes a BLT with a whole pound of bacon. Once, the doctor put me on a diet and the kitchen staff tried to cut back on the bacon, but I fixed that in a hurry.

"Who do you think pays your salary?" I asked, and they nearly broke their necks hustling back to the kitchen for the rest of my bacon.

Now I limp around this mean shack looking for scraps and don't even find a crumb fit for a mouse, let alone a King. Listen, when I get my mojo back, I'll find something to eat. Right now, though, I hear a nap calling my name.

The straw mat on the ground is a far cry from my guitar-shaped silk pillow, but it will have to do.

I'm wallowing in dreams of Pup-Peroni when a little bitty woman with skin like a dried peach pit lifts me off the mat.

"Long lipped god," she says. "Long lipped god."

Well, bless'a my soul. Finally, somebody in this burg recognizes my worth. I'd much prefer to be considered something more glamorous than a god you have to describe as long lipped, but under the current circumstances, any old god will do.

Furthermore, this woman is speaking English, even if it is a fractured version.

Even better, she's got food. She snaps her fingers and six giggling nubile young women with most of their charms hanging out file into the hut and pile food at my feet in pottery dishes.

The food smells like meat and I don't much care what kind. I wolf it down. I'd offer Lovie a bite, but she's surrounded.

It looks like the natives are plying her with drink, and from the way Lovie's eyes are rolling back in her head, I'd say it's a stronger Mayan version of her very own Prohibition Punch.

One of the young women squats beside me and strokes my head while the older woman chants, *Long lipped god.*

I could suggest they call me swivel-hipped god, but considering the alternative (being prodded with spears), I'll take what I can get. If they'd toss in some Pup-Peroni and some visitation privileges with my human mom and dad, I could get used to being a Mayan deity.

There's only one little hitch. I don't know if the natives are priming me like the sacrificial fatted calf, or if they plan to worship at the shrine of the King.

Chapter 11

Motives, Mischief, and Mayhem

While I linger around the Temple of the Frescoes acting as if I intend to spend the rest of the morning sipping coffee and enjoying the sunshine, Mama and Fayrene hotfoot it toward the cliffs to create a diversion.

Mama wouldn't tell me what her diversion will be. She just said, "Leave it to me. We'll meet back at the guest cottage. All you have to do is stick to your plan no matter what you hear." Words that strike terror to my soul. My idea of a diversion is going into a fake faint while Fayrene screams her head off.

They're probably going to do something that will get them arrested. I'll end up spending the rest of my days in the Yucatan dispensing Mexican hairstyles to my new clientele while I try to get Mama and Fayrene out of jail.

Waiting is one of the hardest things for me to do, anyhow, but it's particularly awful with Lovie and Elvis missing and Mama on the loose. I try to sip my coffee, but it has gone cold, so I pretend to be interested in the tourists who have just arrived.

Suddenly, I'm no longer pretending. Lulu Farkle just rounded the corner of the Temple of the Diving God. Did she just step off the ferry from Cozumel or has she been here since last evening, long enough to don a sheet and scare off Rocky's crew, then grab a snake or two and toss them into the bathtub for Fayrene's viewing horror?

And if so, why? What could have possibly gone so horribly wrong between Lovie and Alvin to make his sister resort to kidnapping, ghost impersonation, and almost-murder by snake?

I'm torn between following Lulu to see what she's up to and going forth with my plans to break into Rocky's computer. I have no choice, really. Any minute now Mama and Fayrene will start cutting a ruckus, the diversion angle of our plan.

I sit tight and wait for my opportunity. It's not long in coming. Hard on the heels of Lulu Farkle is a group that includes six teenagers plugged into iPods and cell phones, plus two middle-age women dressed in walking shorts and matching yellow tee shirts that do nothing for their complexions. Both women are wearing plaited plastic lanyards with whistles on the end. Obviously they're in charge, because every few minutes, one of them gives a big toot on the whistle followed by a screech to *stop that, now!*

Breaking and entering just got easier. With this kind of commotion, I don't even need a diversion from Mama. I'm about to head toward the cliffs to tell her when I hear an unholy howl from the sea.

"Haints! Haints!" It can only be Fayrene.

The teenagers bolt for the sea while the leaders huff along behind them, tooting their whistles. Nobody pays them the least bit of attention.

I blend into the melee and am making good progress toward the main cottage when Fayrene screams again.

"Help, somebody, he's throwing Ruby Nell into the sea."

Holy cow! Is Mama going to meet her Maker in the Caribbean or is this the diversion? I'm about to bolt toward the sea when I spot old man Morgan trotting that way. If I'm going to break and enter, now is the time.

Anyhow, Mama's too smart to fall into the Caribbean. Besides, she's got a bucket list two miles long. She's not about to do something foolish that might deprive her of a single adventure.

I wait until Archie Morgan vanishes around the side of the temple, then make a beeline for the main cottage. Thank goodness, the door is unlocked. I can't believe my good luck.

Easing the door open, I slip inside and head straight to Rocky's desk. Without his password, I have no hope of getting into computer files, and the Internet is likely to yield slim pickings on my major suspects. Still, it's worth a try.

It's my lucky day. The computer is up and running.

Since it was his wife's bones Elvis found, I start by typing in Archie Morgan's name. Plus, the man looks like somebody who keeps hatchets under his bed and black widow spiders in his dresser drawer.

The initial search for information on Archie Morgan yields nothing. I'm about to give up on him and move to Alvin and Lulu Farkle when inspiration hits. I type in Morgan's name again, followed by *archeology.*

Bingo. There's an obscure article about a 1965 dig in the Hawaiian Islands led by an archeologist named Archibald Simon Morgan. The dig was fraught with trouble—two cave-ins and four men dead. According to the article, the entire team left the islands in despair and disgrace.

Could it be this Archie? And if so, why isn't he still leading expeditions and searching for hidden treasures? He's probably not much older than Uncle Charlie, and I can't imagine my uncle retiring at any age.

Though the tie-in is suspicious, being an unsuccessful archeologist on a trouble-prone site is not enough to link old man Morgan to anything. Let alone kidnapping and murder.

I type in Alvin Farkle and get an instant hit. An article complete with photograph. Joseph Alvin

Farkle, hairy gorilla arms and all, a famous archeologist in the 30s. He's too old to be Lovie's Farkle. Still, all that hair is a tipoff. Joseph Alvin is bound to be kin.

Suddenly I hear a female voice singing in Spanish. The sound is coming from the direction of the kitchen. Probably Rosita. Somebody ought to tell her it's not appropriate to sing about cockroaches in the kitchen.

I'd do it myself, but I'm standing here with my hand in the cookie jar, so to speak, wondering what I'm going to do if I get caught. Why didn't I check the whereabouts of the cook before I barged in here? Especially after I thought I spotted her outside our cottage following the snake invasion.

Instead of leaving while her boss is gone, as I had assumed, Rosita is still here, most likely cleaning up the breakfast things and making lunch for the skeleton crew (no pun intended) who stayed through the ghost scares to work on Rocky's dig.

Or, is she here for a more diabolical purpose? To spy for whoever kidnapped Lovie? If she really is in love with Rocky, as Lovie claims, then she could easily fall in with a plan to get Lovie out of the way.

Or, does she have some connection to Alvin and Lulu Farkle that I don't know about? Is that why Lulu is here, to confer with Rosita?

I don't have time to stand around wondering. Rosita's liable to come into the living room any minute and demand to know what I'm doing on Rocky's computer. The rest of my life flashes before me. Instead of trying to get Mama out of jail, I'll be in the hoosegow with her. By the time I get out, my eggs will be dead and I won't be far behind.

Holding my breath, I shut off the computer and ease down the lid. Rosita is still warbling, but now she's moving around. Her footsteps echo through the stucco cottage with the finality of a prison cell door slamming shut.

The desk is not in a direct line of sight to the hallway that leads to the kitchen, but by craning my neck I can see her marching this way. With a weapon.

Actually, it's a broom. But in the hands of hatchet-face, it could take my head off with one blow.

Listen, a broom won't compare to a can of Sebastian Shaper Plus Hairspray. Aimed just right, it would stop her cold. Alas, my Shaper Plus is in my tote bag in the guest cottage.

"Señor Rocky? Is that you?"

How am I going to explain my presence? Even if I can, will she listen?

Any second now, she'll come into view and find out it's not her boss. What would Mama do?

Just as the cook comes into sight, I throw

myself on the floor and proceed to have a moaning, writhing, kicking, spitting hissy fit. I'd foam at the mouth if I could, but to pull off that trick, I'd have to have my strawberry scented ultra-foaming shampoo.

Rosita races from the cottage screaming, "*Diablo, diablo!*"

The devil. Listen, I may not be bilingual, but I saw *Romancing the Stone.*

I don't have time to lie on the floor thinking up foreign words. Any minute now Rosita will come back with somebody equipped to deal with the devil. Probably old man Morgan.

Cured of my hissy fit, I get out of there as fast as I can. Thank goodness, I step out of the cottage and into mayhem.

Back at the temple, the teenaged tourists are running wild while the red-faced guides race around tooting their whistles and trying to herd their charges into a circle. I give the milling melee a wide berth as I make my way across the grounds to the guest cottage. The *empty* guest cottage.

Where could Mama and Fayrene be? I search every room calling their names. Their rooms look untouched since our whirlwind pass through to put on clothes after the snake alarm.

I grab my cell phone out of my pocket and try to call Mama, but she's apparently out of range. Where did she go? It would be just like her to be off somewhere channeling her inner animal.

Or worse. Kidnapped.

I hurry out of the cottage and toward the cliffs. Every nerve in my body is twanging. What I want to do is run, screaming. But that would alarm everybody in Tulum, including the tourists.

The whole point of our current investigation is secrecy. We don't want old man Morgan dogging our steps, and I certainly don't want Jack to know what I'm up to.

It's okay for him to traipse around the underbelly of the world getting shot at and no-telling-what-all—or, in this case, traipse through the jungle. But he wants to keep me safe. His very words when I used to beg him to tell me what his profession was. "All I want to do, Cal," he'd say, "is to keep you safe."

If he could, he'd have me under protective custody.

I can't think about that right now. I'm standing on the edge of a cliff searching for missing persons. Specifically, Mama and Fayrene.

There's nothing in sight except a rocky cliff with some occasional scrubby growth, and beyond, an awesome expanse of blue-green water.

I try Mama's cell number again, then Fayrene's, and finally give that up as a lost cause. Walking along the edge of the cliff, I end up at the wall that separates Tulum from the jungle.

The wall I once viewed as picturesque and charming now looks dark and forbidding. Even in broad daylight.

Normally, I'm a nature lover. Back home, I can walk the woods on Mama's farm for hours. But this place makes me want to run and hide under the bed. I don't know if my aversion is due to the jungle itself, or the fact that somewhere out there, Lovie and Elvis are in big trouble.

Maybe Mama and Fayrene, too. I yell for them again.

"Mama? Fayrene?"

"They're not here."

Old man Morgan. I'd know that gravely voice anywhere.

The instinct I call "angels whispering in my ear" says *run*. But my rational self turns to face him and act as if I've spent the entire morning admiring the many scenic views of Tulum instead of trespassing.

Listen, just because somebody reminds you of those creepy old actors who frequently appear in classic horror films starring Bela Lugosi, that doesn't mean he's out to lock you in a dungeon and torture you till you admit your age and weight.

"That's strange." I make myself smile at this old man to show him I mean *strange funny* not *strange scary.* "We were supposed to meet here before lunch."

"They won't be coming. Rocky called and said he and Charlie and Jack wanted to meet the women back at the hotel in Cozumel."

"They've found Lovie and Elvis!" In an instant, Archie Morgan transforms from Lugosi to Matt Damon. Somebody you just want to pat on the head and kiss. Which just goes to show the tricks stress overload can play on you.

"He didn't say, but it sounded like it. I guess they want to surprise you."

"This is wonderful. Where are Mama and Fayrene?"

"Waiting for us down at the ferry. Let's go."

When he takes hold of my arm, I resist the urge to jerk away. He's probably just trying to keep me from stumbling over the uneven ground and taking a fall down the cliff, but maybe he's got a haunted castle around here somewhere and wants to do things to me that involve chains and a hatchet.

A state of panic will benefit no one, least of all me. I force myself to act normal. If there is such a thing. Besides, Jack trusted him enough to put Archie Morgan in charge of watching over us.

Still, I'm not going to just go marching off with a man I don't even halfway trust.

"Wait. I'll need my purse."

"Your mother took care of that. Mighty fine lady, that Miss Ruby Nell."

It's just like Mama to have made another

conquest behind my back, in spite of murder and kidnapping and unknown suspects. I've just barely managed to get Mr. Whitenton, Mama's so-called *dance partner,* out of the picture. I hope I don't have to start all over with old man Morgan.

Out of the blue, I ask, "Do you dance?"

"Never have. Never will."

"Good."

Old man Morgan gives me a funny look, but I don't care. In addition to having babies before my biological clock crashes, my other major goals are taking care of Mama and making sure she doesn't make a crazy mistake that will jeopardize her happiness and the Valentine family farm.

"We need to hurry if we're going to catch the ferry," Morgan says.

Even with his hand on my arm, I begin to relax as we head down the familiar path to the pier. All I have to do is shout and somebody will surely hear. The pier will be crawling with people either unloading to see the ruins of Tulum or waiting to board for the island.

Currently, I see no need to shout except with joy. Now that Lovie and Elvis have been found, we can enjoy Cozumel while Uncle Charlie takes part in the undertakers' convention.

As we leave sight of the ruins, the noise of tourists and the distant hum from the skeleton crew left on the dig fade into silence.

Now that the danger is over, I'm going to fly

home with Elvis so I can make sure Darlene is not running off every client I have at Hair.Net. Just because it took years to build that business doesn't mean it can't be destroyed in a few days.

If I hadn't left it in the hands of somebody I barely know, to travel south of the border, Elvis never would have been kidnapped. Maybe Lovie wouldn't, either. If I hadn't come down here, she might have stayed with Rocky instead of going over to Cozumel for some girl talk with me.

Out of the blue I'm grabbed from behind. Holy cow! In less time than it takes Jack to get me in a compromising position, I'm blindfolded and gagged.

I kick and claw. Judging by the sounds of the grunts and curses, I'm landing some pretty good blows.

The voice muttering off-color words in Lovie's vocabulary is deep. Male, I think. Of course, I could be wrong. I'm not exactly in the ideal position for thinking.

I haul back and swing again, but before I can do further damage with my fingernails, my hands are bound behind my back, and I'm shoved into a thicket where brambles proceed to mutilate me.

What about Archie Morgan? Is he captive, too, or is he in on the kidnapping?

And what about Mama and Fayrene? Are they waiting at the pier, or have they been kidnapped, too?

There's no way I'm going to fight my way out of this situation. Besides, I need to save my strength for the heavy chains and sharp axes in my immediate future. Maybe even stewpots and cannibals. I don't want to think about it right now.

I stop my useless struggle and try to learn what I can by listening.

The only sounds I hear are bird calls and the rustling of bushes as I'm half shoved, half dragged wherever my kidnapper is taking me.

If I'm lucky, I'll end up in the same place as Lovie and Elvis. Listen, whoever this criminal is, he'd better watch out. When I get together with my cousin and my dog, there's no stopping us. Even unarmed, we're dangerous.

And I don't even want to think about what Jack Jones will do when he discovers I'm missing.

Elvis' Opinion #9 on Gods, Captivity, and Blue Suede Shoes

I could get accustomed to this life as a god. Though I'd still prefer to be a major and more glamorous deity like Quetzalcoatl, I'm discovering more and more advantages to being the long lipped god.

For one thing, nothing is expected of me. I've been in this hut all day long lolling on a mat while the natives bring me food. Furthermore, every little move I make is imitated. When I get up to take a piss, the natives trail along behind to do the same thing. When I shake myself all over just to hear the tag on my handsome pink dog collar—a move I'm very fond of because it reminds me of my swivel-hipped days onstage at Las Vegas—everybody in the village gathers round and starts shaking.

The next thing I know, they'll all show up in my hut wearing the Mayan equivalent of a dog collar.

Except for worrying how Callie is handling my absence, and missing my human mom and dad, I'm faring fine in the jungle.

I wish I could say the same thing about Lovie. I still can't figure out what they intend to be her fate. Around noon, they started plying her with food, too, but they're keeping her so drunk on their Mayan version of Long Island Iced Tea, she's unable to question the one person in this joint who speaks English, sort of.

Even with my radar ears and superior powers of deduction, I'm unable to find out anything because everywhere I go, I have a huge following. If I weren't still running around in this dog suit, I'd think I was in Las Vegas with fans clamoring just to get near me. One of the best times I ever had was the night I wore my black gypsy outfit and the chain on my thousand-dollar belt broke. I just laughed about it and gave pieces of it to my adoring fans. That was also the night I sang "Young and Beautiful," and somebody in the audience yelled, "Elvis, you're beautiful."

I guess I was. I never thought about it. My mama (Gladys) raised me to be humble.

And I guess I still am. In spite of the misinformed opinions of the judges at the dog shows I've entered, and my slightly mismatched ears, which you'd hardly notice if you didn't pick them up and look closely, I've seen enough reflections of myself in Callie's beauty shop mirrors to know that I'm a one-in-a-million, over-the-top handsome basset.

Well, judge for yourself. What other basset could end up in the jungle being worshipped by the natives? If I can get them completely caught up in imitating me, maybe I can slip away unnoticed and try to find my way back to Tulum.

I'm sure Charlie's called in Jack and they've got search parties everywhere. But they could use a little help from a highly placed deity. Namely, a basset god.

I stand up, stretch a bit, then do a few of my famous pelvis moves. This really gets the natives going. They're gyrating all over the place, laughing, and trying to match my every swivel.

Next I launch into a fabulous basset edition of "Blue Suede Shoes." Instead of being totally transported by my music and my moves, they scratch their heads a bit, then all throw back their heads and start howling.

"That's All Right Mama." Obviously the song that made blue suede the most famous footwear in the world is totally wrong for barefoot natives.

"Shake, Rattle and Roll" ought to do the trick. I'm fixing to light into a rousing rendition when I'm cut off from my audience by five women rushing by. And every last one of them is pregnant.

Without pausing to listen to my concert, they rush into the hut where Lovie's in no condition to do anything except moan.

"Don't Ask Me Why." Even in my current god status, I don't have a clue what's going on.

But leave it to the King to find out. I bow to my audience and they all bow right back. Then I prance my well-fed self into the hut to find out Lovie's fate.

Chapter 12

Desperate Measures and Danger from a Dark-Eyed Stranger

In my current condition (bound, gagged, and blindfolded), the only thing I can tell about where I'm going is that it's back uphill.

I try to judge the time by counting silently. By the time my captor shoves me over some kind of threshold, I judge it has taken us about the same length of time to reach this place as it took for me to leave Tulum and walk into this trap.

The place smells of dust motes, dirty clothes, and fried oysters. I sincerely hope that's not my lunch. If God made a mistake, it was oysters. They have to be the worst, slimiest, most vile-tasting food on this earth. Of course, if anything could make up for the mistake, though, it's the pearls.

"Move." That sounds like a female voice. Do I have two captors?

I catch a whiff of faintly familiar perfume. Where have I smelled that before? The undertakers' convention breakfast? Lulu Farkle?

If the Farkles think Lovie did something outrageous to Alvin, they might want to get revenge on her. But why me?

I am shoved hard and end up on a mattress so thin I can feel the bedsprings poking through. Before I can land a good kick, my legs are trussed together and my hands unbound, then handcuffed to a metal bedpost.

If my current treatment is any indication, I can quit worrying about oysters: I won't be having lunch today. Maybe not even dinner.

"You'll be sorry." My threat loses some power through the gag, but that doesn't stop me. "Wait till Uncle Charlie and Jack finish with you."

There's the sound of laughter. Definitely female.

"Search her." That male voice again. It sounds familiar but I can't place it. Probably because my blood sounds like the Pacific surf surging through my ears, rough hands are all over me going through my pockets and jerking out my cell phone, and I'm scared out of my mind.

Then I hear footsteps heading back toward the door. Definitely two people. Maybe more.

What next? One thing's for sure. I don't plan to lie still and wait for my kidnappers to turn me into the next set of bones discovered at Tulum.

I work my mouth, trying to loosen the gag so I can scream, but all I achieve is chafing my skin.

"Lovie! Elvis!" This comes through my gag sounding like *Mmmmfee, Eeefis.*

Wait a minute. Did I hear voices? Straining, I make out what seems to be the distant chatter of children. Are they playing nearby? Can they hear me if I make enough commotion?

I rattle my handcuffs against the metal bedpost and scream muffled bloody murder. Nobody— let alone a group of children—charges to my rescue.

Holy cow! What did I expect? At the rate I'm going, I'll be hoarse and voiceless in two hours. Not to mention chafed and bruised.

The sounds are still filtering through. I get quiet so I can make them out. The chatter seems to be increasing in volume, but I can't understand what they're saying.

Wait a minute. Are those whistles I hear? Suddenly I remember the group touring Tulum, all those milling, unruly teenagers and the two leaders frantically tooting their whistles.

What in the world is going on? The whistles shrill once more, then the chatter fades and ceases.

I wait and wait, but hear nothing more. Sweat rolls from under my thick hair and down my cheeks. I'm thirsty and hungry. Not to mention the fact that I could use a bathroom break, and there's a creature crawling in this bed that I hope is not a tarantula.

I picture him the size of my front porch rocking chair, getting ready to wrap his hairy legs around me and start gnawing with teeth that look like a crosscut saw. I wonder if overexcitement can kill a person my age. Since I'm not ready to give up and die, childless, I force myself to think about something nice. Mama's farm. The cool blue lake. The low-hanging oak tree limb Lovie and I used as a childhood swing.

Heat and fear are taking their toll. The last thing I remember is thinking about the way you can play hooky on a quiet Sunday morning, sit on that low-hanging limb of the oak in the pasture on Mama's farm, and still hear gospel music from the Wildwood Baptist Church just across the little two-lane country Highway 371.

• • •

"Callie?" I bolt out of my faint. "Where are you?"

That's Mama! What in the world's going on here?

"Yahoo. Callie!" Fayrene's voice. This is weird. "I guess she got irrigated when she found out we took the ferry without her."

That's definitely Fayrene. Sounding as if she's in the next room. Which is impossible. If they had been kidnapped, they'd be bound and gagged, too. And they certainly wouldn't be talking as if nothing out of the ordinary had happened.

"Callie's not like that." Mama says, defending me. I don't know why, but this makes me feel better.

"Well, Darlene would have been mad enough to chomp ten-penny nails about missing out on the voodoo shop in Cozumel."

They've been shopping?

"Let's stow our costumes in our room so we can hide the ceremonial stuff at the temple before the men get back."

Holy cow! Mama and Fayrene are in the guest cottage. Which means the kidnappers have planted bugs all over Tulum. That explains why I heard voices and whistles earlier.

It also means that whoever did the kidnapping has unlimited access not only to Tulum but to all the buildings used by the team of archeologists. Plus, whoever planted the bugs had a better than passing knowledge of electronics.

When Lovie was dating Farkle, didn't I hear her say his sister used to be some kind of surveillance expert?

There's the sound of rustling followed by footsteps. Electronic, not real. Then, silence. I wait awhile, but hear nothing more.

When will Mama discover I'm missing? And why isn't she worried?

If Archie told them the same thing he told me, then obviously Uncle Charlie met Mama and Fayrene in Cozumel, and Lovie is okay. But if she's okay, why are the men still in the jungle? And why are Mama and Fayrene planning a ceremony that involves costumes and no-telling-what-all?

Or maybe Archie Morgan didn't send Fayrene and Mama to the island. Maybe they evaded his watchful eye and went on their own. But why would they go without telling me?

The more I try to untangle the mystery, the more twisted it becomes.

My stomach growls and my bladder sends distress signals. I don't know which will happen first—I'll die of hunger or I'll explode.

Either way, if I don't take some desperate measures, I'm destined to become a tragic Marilyn Monroe figure, cut down in my prime, leaving Champ to yearly pilgrimages to put roses on my crypt and Jack to repent of buying a Harley Screamin' Eagle with heated seats instead of a baby cradle.

I should have listened to Bobby Huckabee. The next time he predicts *danger from a dark-eyed stranger,* I won't be caught without my gun.

Or at least an extra large can of Sebastian Shaper Plus.

Elvis' Opinion #10 on Pregnancy, Pup-Peroni, and Jungle Protocol

Well, bless'a my soul. What do I discover but Lovie sitting on her jungle throne, still half-crocked, while a bevy of pregnant natives bow at her feet. They're chanting something, but even with my famous ears, it takes me awhile to figure it out.

"Ixchel, Ixchel."

An ordinary dog wouldn't have a clue what that means, but you're dealing with the King. When I was so famous I couldn't go anywhere without being mobbed, I spent a lot of time holed up in my bedroom reading. After I'd gone through every novel that caught my fancy, I started in on the encyclopedia. Read every volume from A to Z.

And I still remember it all. What did you expect from a musical genius who in his other life could hear a song one time, then sit down at the piano and sing it back, word for word and note for note?

These women believe Lovie is the Earth and Moon goddess. What they want from Ixchel/ Lovie is anybody's guess.

If it's help birthing their babies, I've got news for them. Unless they stop giving their new goddess that native potion powerful enough to knock a bull elephant off its feet, they're going to have to depend on somebody else to bring all those little Mayan babies into this world.

I just hope it's not yours truly. But if it is, the King is up to any challenge. My manager's brother-in-law once said the secret to being Elvis was always being polite and appreciative. That was true in my other life, and it's still true now. Every time Callie gives me some Pup-Peroni, I lick her hands.

But the real secret to being Elvis is a generosity of spirit that flows from me straight into the hearts of everybody around me.

Listen, if any one of these little pregnant girls needs a long lipped god to help her bring her baby into the world, then I'm just the dog to "Take Good Care of Her."

The mommies-to-be haven't noticed me yet, so I sneak into the corner where I can watch, unobserved. If these natives see me, they'll rush over and transfer their loyalties to the long lipped god who knows how to teach them to move a "Heart of Stone."

I understand jungle protocol. Let every god have his day.

It's Lovie's turn. Besides, it's time to quit messing around enjoying the glory of god-dom and figure out if she's their goddess sacrifice or their goddess oracle.

If Lovie's an intended sacrifice, I've got to have "Just a Little Talk with Jesus." Then I've got to have a plan.

Chapter 13

Complications, Hot Tempers, and Prohibition Punch

Right before I pass out from trying to keep from embarrassing myself, one of my captors comes back, unshackles me, unties my legs, pokes a gun into my ribs and says, "Move. And don't think about trying anything."

His voice is muffled. He's probably wearing a mask or a cloth over his mouth. I don't know whether he's disguising his voice because he's somebody I know, or whether this is a simple precaution.

After a few steps, he pulls open a door with squeaky hinges. "Bathroom. You've got five seconds and I've got a gun."

I'm so relieved, I couldn't execute an escape plan even if I had one. I lift my blindfold, then wish I hadn't. If I found a public restroom this dirty back home, I'd leave and suggest Scrubbing Bubbles to the management. Plus, there's no window in it.

I finish my business as fast as I can, pull my blindfold back into place, then hand myself back over to my kidnapper. I briefly consider lifting my head to see if I can catch a glimpse of him from underneath the bottom of the blindfold, but quickly discard the foolhardy notion. If he knows I can identify him, I'm dead. And I'd really rather live out the rest of my life dispensing New York hairdos to Mooreville's glitterati and rescuing stray cats and dogs than die in a dirty jungle shack that smells like oysters.

We march back to the bed where he shackles my hands to the bedpost.

"Try getting out of that, Houdini."

My captor walks off, leaving my legs unbound. Thank goodness.

Did he forget or are my kidnappers so confident I can't escape that it doesn't matter? The door slams behind him and I am alone. Except for that creepy, crawly thing in my bed, which I'm not even going to think about.

It must be evening by now. Earlier, I tried to keep track of time by counting, but my unexpected nap threw me off. Still, my hunger alone tells me I've been here for hours.

Also, the kidnapper who took me to the bathroom sounded like the same one who brought me here. That probably means he lives or is staying nearby. Either in Tulum or on the island. Which brings me back to the Farkles. Or old man Morgan, who seems to be at the center of everything.

Suddenly, I hear Fayrene's voice again.

"Ruby Nell, do you think the chicken blood is enough?"

Enough for what? I'm wondering.

"It'll have to do. We don't have time to go out into the jungle and hunt down a wild pig."

"I couldn't suffice a pig, anyhow. I don't even eat bacon."

Holy cow! Mama and Fayrene are planning a clandestine sacrifice. That must mean Lovie and Elvis are still missing. Or they've discovered I'm missing. If so, why is Mama not hysterical?

Suddenly the bugs pick up all kinds of commotion—footsteps, male voices all talking at once, Mama and Fayrene saying something I don't quite catch. The hubbub builds, then subsides. There are more footsteps and I hear Uncle Charlie.

"Is everybody here?"

"Seth's still at the dig checking on the remnants of my crew." Rocky sounds tired and sad, like he's barely hanging on. "Let's go ahead without him. I can bring him up to speed later."

"Where's Callie?" Jack. I can picture him, head and shoulders above everybody else, scanning the group for me.

Obviously, the main cottage is also bugged, since that's the gathering place of choice for the Valentine summits.

"She wasn't in the guest cottage." Mama, sounding a bit worried. "I thought she'd be here."

For a while I can't hear anything. Then Jack says, "She doesn't answer her phone. When did you last see her, Ruby Nell?"

He's got that hard edge in his voice, which is the only outward sign that he's disturbed.

I can almost see Mama's wheels turning. She's probably trying to figure out how to tell Jack where she last saw me without revealing what we were up to.

"I believe it was at the Temple of the Frescoes, sometime this morning."

"What time?" Jack again.

"Let's see. I think it was around tenish or so. Do you remember, Fayrene?"

"I remember exactly. I have a pornographic memory. It was twenty-five minutes after ten."

"You mean you haven't seen Callie all day?"

"Jack, let me handle this." Uncle Charlie, trying to calm Jack down. "Ruby Nell, if Callie left Tulum, you have to tell us."

"She wouldn't know." I'm almost positive that voice belongs to old man Morgan. "Miss Ruby Nell and Mrs. Johnson have been gone most of the day."

"You were supposed to keep an eye on the women here." Uncle Charlie sounds ready to shoot somebody.

"They did a big favor for me today," Archie says. "Between the ghosts and the search for Miss Lovie, we're shorthanded around here. Miss Ruby Nell and Mrs. Johnson kindly agreed to pick up some supplies for dinner in Cozumel."

Shivers run over me. Archie Morgan's the kidnapper. If not the main one, then he's certainly in on it.

His announcement creates chaos. Everybody starts talking at once—angry voices, some shouting. I can't make out a thing.

Morgan's machinations would explain why Mama was not upset when she and Fayrene returned from Cozumel this afternoon. He got them out of the way, then lied to me so I would leave Tulum with him.

He was probably responsible for Lovie's kidnapping, too. But why? And who are his cohorts?

My money is still on the Farkles. At least Alvin. The female accomplice could be that weird maid who changes sheets in the middle of the night. Juanita. But how are they all connected?

Fayrene's voice blares through the hidden microphones. "Jarvetis, everybody's getting hijacked right and left down here." She must be standing next to a hidden bug, calling home. "First Lovie and Elvis and now Callie. I could be next. I'm just in a state of constitution."

Well, I guess she is in a state of consternation. Mama, too, who suddenly screams, "Jack, you find my baby!"

"Don't worry, Ruby Nell. I'll find her. Whoever took Cal had better wish he were dead."

From Jack Jones, that's not a threat, that's a promise. I wonder who else heard him. If old man Morgan is still in the main cottage, I hope he's having second thoughts. I hope he's planning to come to this dingy shack—wherever it is—and turn me loose.

There's another long stretch of chaotic, indecipherable sounds and then silence. Jack's not going to wait to see if I turn up or bother depending on the authorities. If I know him—and I blush to think how well I do—he's storming around Tulum right this minute searching for clues to my disappearance.

I'd guess it's dark now, and that will hamper him, but it won't stop him. Jack will find me.

If I don't figure a way out of here myself first.

The door bangs against the wall and one of my captors stomps across the room. It doesn't take me long to find out who.

"I guess you heard the show. If you're smart, you've already put two and two together and come up with me."

Old man Morgan rips off my blindfold and then my gag. Let me tell you, if you thought my screams over the snakes were loud, you ought to hear me now.

Archie Morgan's laugh makes my skin crawl. "Be my guest. Scream your head off. Nobody can hear you."

"Why not, you backside of a barnyard animal?" Lovie would have been more specific. "Did you take my cousin, too? Is she alive?"

"Let me see now. That's three questions. Which one should I answer first?" His cackle reminds me of the evil stepmother from *Snow White*. Listen, I'll admit it. I still love Walt Disney.

"I just can't figure it out," Archie adds, "so I won't answer any of them."

"Wait till my husband finds you." I blame the shackles for my small slip of the tongue. "You'll be a greasy spot in the road."

"I'm shaking in my boots." Archie Morgan marches out of the room, whistling, obviously pleased with himself.

"Come back here, you piece of toad snot. I'm not through with you. Why can't anybody hear me?"

Even if Archie Morgan left the main cottage

171

before Fayrene called Jarvetis, it still took him only a few minutes to get here. Which means I'm probably in the caretaker's shack. I remember seeing it on a rocky bluff overlooking Tulum. Close enough for somebody to hear.

I scream again, but nobody comes rushing to my rescue. Morgan's probably got this thing soundproofed. Which means he'd been planning Lovie's kidnapping for a long time or he's done this before.

I'm not the kind of woman who wastes time engaging in useless behavior. I climb off my screaming high horse and settle down to use my brain.

Morgan's liable to take a notion to blindfold me again, so the first thing I do is look around. There are monitors hanging all over the walls, all showing views of Tulum. I can see every room in the guest and the main cottages, plus every structure in the ruins, inside and out. There are even several viewpoints of Rocky's dig. Morgan and his cohorts have been thorough.

I can hear him moving around in the next room, still whistling.

"Who's helping you?" I yell.

"Wouldn't you like to know?"

"I already do."

"Then why'd you ask?"

He has a point. I blame lack of food for my brain malfunction.

172

"Did you bring Lulu and Alvin Farkle in on the kidnapping, or did they enlist you?"

"Keep up that smartmouth talk and you won't get any supper."

Supper is a distinctly Southern term. Know your enemy. That's my new motto.

"What part of the South are you from?"

Morgan doesn't answer. I can't remember whether Rocky mentioned Morgan's origins. If he did, it would have been before the caretaker mattered.

Suddenly I spot Mama and Fayrene on one of the monitors, entering the guest cottage.

"I can't believe it! My daughter, taken!"

"Lord, Ruby Nell. Are you fixing to have a prostration attack?"

"No! I've got things to do. Get me some of Lovie's Prohibition Punch."

Fayrene goes to the refrigerator. "It's gone."

"What do you mean, it's gone? Don't tell me they've kidnapped Lovie's punch, too!"

"If pornographic memory serves, you drank the last drop, Ruby Nell."

"Well, make some more."

"I don't know the recipe."

Mama storms to the refrigerator and grabs a bottle of vodka. "Brew some tea, Fayrene. This will do."

Watching them go about the ordinary ritual of making tea, then the uniquely Mama and Fayrene ritual of adding vodka, I get teary-eyed. If I were there, we'd be arguing over whatever plans Mama has for the chicken blood. Good-naturedly, of course. Mama and I have never really been mad at each other. She blusters and I bluff, but deep down, we're each other's best friend. Which is what mothers and daughters ought to be.

I wonder if I'll live to find out what that's like.

In the next room, Morgan is making all kinds of sounds—chairs scraping the floor, feet stomping around, drawers opening and slamming shut, cutlery rattling.

That doesn't sound like supper preparations to me. I'd shout back there and ask him, but I think you can push these bad guys only so far before they turn really vicious.

Until lately, my contact with bad guys was limited mostly to watching late-night TV classics with Lovie. But since my cousin and I have been turning up corpses with some regularity recently, I'm coming to learn more about walking on the wild side than I ever wanted to know.

Based on my recent experience with murder in Memphis, I shudder to think what Morgan's skullduggery back there with the cutlery is all about. Did he kill his wife, then cut her into small pieces and bury her bones in Tulum? Holy cow, am I his next victim?

Elvis' Opinion #11 on Clever Plans, Escape Route, and the Church of Lovie

I still can't figure out what's going on. The only person in this village who speaks English has left our hut, and the little pregnant women are doing "What Every Woman Lives For." They're over there by Lovie's throne conducting a beauty ritual.

When they filed in here, I didn't know what was in those tiny pots they were holding. Makeup, what else? They've smeared it all over Lovie. She now looks so much like a jungle tigress that you could have fooled me—that is, if I were a silly shih tzu, or a ridiculous Lhasa apso who thinks he's the Dalai Lama.

This must be phase two of whatever ritual the natives have in mind. They're either readying her for the stewpot or getting ready to worship at the church of Lovie.

I'd worship there, myself. Fat, sugar, and alcohol—the food and drink of choice—and *live large,* the only commandment.

Still, if this is a stewpot prelude, I'd better shake my slightly crooked hind leg and launch into phase one of my own plan.

If "We're Gonna Move" out of here, I've got to shag my long lipped godly self out of here and stake out an escape route through the jungle. The mothers-to-be are so busy decking Lovie out in a feathered headdress and a costume that reveals more flesh than even Lovie is comfortable showing, they'll never know I've gone.

I don't want Lovie worrying, though. I do a swivel-hipped dance so she'll "Turn Around and Look at Me," but she's so deep in her cups from all that Mayan brew they've been giving her, she wouldn't notice if I were standing in the corner doing a bad imitation of Johnny Cash singing "Folsom Prison Blues."

If we don't get out of here, I'll be singing "Mayan Prison Blues." I hurry outside and do a verse of "Swing Down Sweet Chariot," hoping old Abe will get the picture and swing on down from the trees for the first leg of Mission Rescue.

Wouldn't you know, when there's real work to be done, that monkey's off eating bananas. Which reminds me of the good old days back in Graceland, and more recently at my home in Mooreville, when I could have a fried peanut butter and banana sandwich no matter what time of night I took a hankering.

It'll be dark soon. I can't stand here all day waiting for a goofy monkey to do a dog's work. Abe doesn't know what he's missing. If he'd help me, I had planned to have some necklaces made kind of like I did in the glory days when I wore pants with only two legs. Only these wouldn't say TCB (Taking Care of Business); they'd say ECDL (Elvis and Company, Detectives at Large.)

Monkeyless, I set out toward the jungle with my nose to the ground. Listen, this is a famous nose. It doesn't take me long to pick up the scent. Which means I can find our way back to the shack where Lovie was first held hostage. Once I'm there, it won't take me long to pick up the scent of our kidnapper.

If anybody's "Ready Teddy" to blow this joint, it's me. I'm fed up with being a long lipped god.

Besides, there's no telling what that uppity Lhasa apso has been up to in my absence. It would be just like him to try to take complete command at Hair.Net. Listen, that's my domain. No sawed-off dog with a bushy tail is going to usurp the King.

If I let him get away with that, the next thing you know, he'll be trying to steal my guitar-shaped pillow and take over my favorite pissing post in the beauty shop's yard. Then it'll be my personal stash of Pup-Peroni and the ham bones I've got seasoning in strategic burial grounds— in case I get a sneak snack attack while Callie's touching up Fayrene's roots and trying to talk Mama into forgoing a gambling jaunt to Las Vegas.

It's time to snatch back my sneer, break out my swivel, and go back to being the King.

Chapter 14

Ghostly Encounters, Tiger by the Tail, and Beauty to the Rescue

While I'm still worrying about being stripped and filleted by Archie Morgan's knives, his cell phone rings. Mama and Fayrene are no longer on the guest cottage monitor, and all the others are blank, so I don't have any trouble hearing Morgan's end of the conversation. And let me tell you, I'm all ears.

The first thing I hear is my kidnapper's screech of outrage.

"She what? How could you let her do that?"

They can't be talking about me. I haven't done anything. Are they talking about Mama? She inspires outrage with a frequency that would give me high blood pressure if I didn't have a front porch swing and a good dog to cuddle. I know that sounds simplistic, but let me tell you, sometimes a loyal dog can be better than a husband, a best friend, and a therapist all rolled into one.

"You should have handcuffed her," Morgan rages on. "You've got to find her before Rocky does."

Lovie! It has to be. I cry with relief, though if she were here, she'd say, *Buck up and stop that. You've got things to do.*

I'm not surprised she escaped. Listen, if she'd had her baseball bat, my cousin would have beat the tar out of anybody who messed with her.

In the next room, old man Morgan says, "If she was smart enough to get away, she might be smart enough to survive the jungle. Get that witch. If he gets to her first, we can kiss our plans goodbye."

If Lovie can escape, so can I. The only question is, how?

"All right, calm down." I wish Morgan would say a name, so I'd know who he's talking to. "As long as we've got the other one, we're still in control."

Not for long, mister. With Lovie and Elvis on the loose, your goose is cooked.

"I'll handle the ghosts myself. The two of you go after the redheaded witch."

Old man Morgan slams around in the next room, muttering words in Lovie's vocabulary (but not mine, thank goodness). When he finally comes into the room I'm in, he's carrying a white sheet and a plate of food that smells like something I'm not about to eat.

"So Lovie outsmarted you and your partners."

"Not for long. And I've still got you, girlie."

"Why are you doing this?"

Morgan looks at me like I've sprouted extra ears, and his face undergoes more transformations than Mama's hair. He's either so mad about my audacious question that he's going to slice my throat on the spot, or he's going to laugh his head off. To my surprise, he does neither.

"I've been searching for the lost tomb of the Nine Lords for years. Why do you think I took this dead-end job?"

I've read that kidnappers and their victims sometimes develop a close relationship. Heaven help me. Still, I leap to take advantage of my new role as Morgan's confidante.

"So you kidnapped Lovie and ran Rocky's men off with ghosts to distract him from the dig so you could go in, finish the work he'd started, and then claim credit for his discovery?"

"I'm not about to let Rocky Malone walk away with the glory. By the time I finish with him, he'll wish he'd never set foot on Tulum."

"All this surveillance equipment. You've done this before."

Instantly his face transforms from Morgan the Sociable to Morgan the Terrible.

"You think you're so smart. Wait till I finish with you."

He sounds so mean I almost wet my pants. Listen, I may display occasional flashes of valor, but deep down, I'm a girly girl who prefers pink polish to the red badge of courage.

"You won't get away with murder."

"Who said anything about murder? Maybe I've got something worse in mind."

Holy cow! I wish I'd read some books on criminal psychology. When you're faced with possible torture by snakes and other methods too diabolical to think about, is it better to act brave or to be weak and complacent?

Too late now. I've already stepped off the sidewalk and into deep doodoo, as Lovie would say. Only she'd use more earthy language.

When Morgan heads my way, I see my chance to drop him and get the keys to my handcuffs. Listen, that fool who led me to the bathroom was so busy congratulating himself that I couldn't summon help from a soundproof shack, he forgot that long, limber legs can be lethal weapons.

When Morgan sets my plate of odious prison food on the floor, I put all the power of my five feet and nine inches of pure outrage into my kick. Right to his groin.

With a howl, he clutches himself, then dances around screaming in a high-pitched voice.

Meantime, I see my plan to drop him to the floor and then get his keys as not only half-baked, but also suicidal. How did I think I was going to get them, anyway? Both hands are cuffed to the bedpost. And I'd rather face snakes with a Jimmy Choo stiletto than retrieve anything from old man Morgan's pockets with my mouth.

He recovers enough to call me names that are not even in Lovie's vocabulary.

"You've just deprived yourself of supper, girlie." He snatches up the plate.

"What can I say? 'When I get excited about something, I give it all I've got.'" Lauren Bacall in *Dark Passage.*

If Lovie were here, she'd have guessed that. When she's not trying to put love handles on me with her home cooking, she's bringing movie classics to my house so we can ogle the Lone Ranger in his mask and learn to speak the language of film noir from Humphrey Bogart.

Old man Morgan hobbles out of the room and returns with enough hardware to shackle everyone in Fort Knox. He's also bearing a piece of bread. Either it's his midnight, posthaunting snack or it's my dinner.

He proceeds to cuff my ankles together, then frees my left hand and slaps the bread in it. After making sure my right wrist is still securely shackled to the bed, he hobbles out without another word. Still carrying his sheet.

Under other circumstances, I wouldn't eat a bite his slimy hands have touched, but it so happens I'm starving to death. Thankful to have at least one hand free, I nibble a few bites, then brush back the hair that has tumbled out of my hasty hairstyle and into my face.

Holy cow! Hairpins. My French twist is full of them. My meager supper forgotten, I reach up and pluck the key to my escape.

Old man Morgan had better beware of a hairstylist wielding a hairpin. If I can't get it to open my handcuffs, I'll use it to poke his eyes out.

I'm not a lefty, and it's awkward trying to pick the lock that secures my right hand to the bedpost. Plus, I wish I could have a redo and learn everything Slick Fingers Johnson taught Lovie. Listen, when I get back home, I'm going to learn so much about self-defense, folks in Mooreville will have to call me Rambo-etta.

Sound crackles through the speakers, and when I glance up at the monitors, I see Archie Morgan haunting the sleeping quarters of Rocky's crew. Somebody ought to tell him that saying "Wooo, wooo" won't scare anybody.

Within minutes, the remnants of Rocky's crew streak out of bed and across the compound, proving me dead wrong. With Archie Morgan chasing them in a sheet, everyone in the crew races past the ruins of ancient temples, then they leap over the wall and into the jungle where I can no longer see them. If their earlier flight pattern is any indication, they won't stop running till daylight.

Poor Rocky. Now he's left with nobody on his crew except Seth and Archie.

Where is Lovie's almost-lover, anyhow? And Uncle Charlie and Jack?

I redouble my efforts to pick the lock. Somebody needs to tell them that Archie Morgan is a traitor and a kidnapper. Also, somebody needs to tell them that Lovie has escaped and is alive.

Well, I hope she still is. I shudder to think about my cousin and Elvis trying to find their way out of a snake-infested jungle. With cannibals, too, for all I know.

Listen, murder and kidnapping are serious business. We're not in the middle of *Raiders of the Lost Ark* here. Harrison Ford a.k.a. Indiana Jones is not going to jump out of the bushes any minute and subdue the bad guys with his famous whip and his lethal smile.

There's Jack, of course. But where is he? Without Indiana Jones, I redouble my efforts with the hairpin.

On the monitor I see old man Morgan picking his way among the temples. Before you know it, he'll be back and my clandestine activities will come to a halt.

Wait a minute. What's this I see? I squint to pick up the night-shrouded images on the monitor. It looks like some kind of native ritual taking place on the steps of the temple of She of the Jade-Green Skirts. One of the natives is wearing a feathered headdress that reminds me of the one Lovie wore undercover as Las Vegas' most outrageous showgirl. A towering affair that looks as if it will topple at any minute. The other has on a birdlike mask of some sort that features a lethal-looking beak.

I wouldn't want to meet either one of them in the dark. And I certainly wouldn't want to be part of what they're preparing to do at the temple. Human sacrifice, it looks like.

The one with the headdress bends down to light candles and her face can be seen. A painted-on tiger face, jet black hair, a movie star cigarette holder in her mouth.

Holy cow! It's Mama, channeling her inner animal, no doubt. Obviously the long-beaked bird is Fayrene, her major cohort in crime and all things designed to give me early gray hairs.

My suspicions are confirmed when she starts chanting her grocery list.

"Man-goes, pa-pa-ya, kum-quat."

"Fayrene, are those fruits?"

"Yeah, Ruby Nell, but they're erotic fruits."

Exotic, I think, but who knows? Anything that works.

Apparently Mama is satisfied, because while Fayrene chants, she sprinkles some kind of liquid all over the temple steps. Chicken blood? I don't even want to know.

Suddenly I spot somebody else in the monitor. Old man Morgan, still in his sheet, headed toward the temple and on a collision course with Mama and Fayrene.

"Watch out, Mama," I scream, for all the good it will do.

Still, who knows the powers of the bond

between mother and daughter? I think they could be stronger than the pull of the moon. As if to prove my theory, Mama looks up and spots old man Morgan.

"Scream, Mama," I yell at the monitor. "Call Uncle Charlie."

"Fayrene!" Mama yells. "The spell's working!"

As usual, she ignores my advice. Might I also add, she's elated? Mama loves nothing better than being right in the thick of things, and, lately, murder has provided her with plenty of opportunities.

Streaking down the steps with the spryness of a teenager, she yells at the now rapidly fleeing ghost, "Come back here, you devil."

I have to say, I'm proud of her.

"You go, Mama."

Listen, if being decked out like a tiger can make Mama act twenty years younger, I might introduce finding-your-inner-animal makeup to my clients at Hair.Net.

Fayrene is not far behind Mama. "Stop, you sperm of Satin."

I think she means spawn of Satan, but I could be wrong. With a ritual like the one they're performing, anything goes.

Morgan is easily outdistancing them. I shut my eyes and wish every bit of the bad karma he's dispensed comes back to him. I know that's not nice, but he's not a nice man.

When he trips on his sheet, I let out a very unladylike rebel yell.

Mama and Fayrene catch up to him and pounce. "Unmask the imposter," Mama yells.

"Haints begone!" Fayrene screams.

They begin a fierce tug-of-war over the sheet, two against one, while old man Morgan struggles to regain his footing.

I'm betting on Mama and Fayrene.

I give a few more rebel yells and some of my best high school cheers. I make bargains with God and St. Jude and St. Joseph Aspirin. Listen, if it would help end this horrible ordeal, I'd promise to give up cute shoes and sex with my ex.

If I weren't half-starved and in shackles and facing a fate worse than death, I'd be enjoying the best show in town.

My hairpin forgotten, I hold my breath as the three of them struggle in the dark.

"Yell for Jack," I scream at the monitor. "Call Uncle Charlie."

Obviously they don't hear me. Nobody can.

Old man Morgan screams, "Let go, you hags from hell!"

"Who are you calling a hag, you coward?" Mama hauls off and socks him in the face.

Morgan staggers backward, but regains his footing so fast I'm wondering if he's kin to my feisty little cat, Happy.

"Now, Mama! Go after him."

She's raring back to land him another blow when Morgan lowers his head and plows into Fayrene. The blow knocks her sideways into Mama, and they topple in a heap of feathers, war paint, and chicken blood.

From her position underneath Fayrene, Mama yells, "Don't let him get away."

"I've got him." Fayrene grabs and ends up with a fistful of thin air.

Meanwhile, Morgan makes his getaway, his sheet and his hidden identity still intact.

It won't be long before he returns to the mean shack. And let me tell you, he's going to be madder than he was when he left. Mama has that effect.

And it doesn't help that I kicked him in his privates.

There's no telling what kind of revenge he'll exact on me.

Getting a good grip on my hairpin, I redouble my escape efforts. Listen, this is hard work. For one thing, using my left hand is awkward. For another, I'm no hardened criminal who goes around the neighborhood picking locks.

In desperation, I call on Mother Earth, Mother Teresa, and motherhood. If I thought it would help, I'd chant Fayrene's erotic fruit list.

Chapter 15

Breadcrumbs, Inner Animals, and Wild Goose Chases

When Morgan roars back into the shack, I barely have time to hide my hairpin. I guess that's the point of sound-proofed shacks. Your victims can't be heard screaming, and they can't hear you coming.

I try my best to look innocent, but apparently I'm not the object of Morgan's interest. He stops in front of the monitors, then stands there mesmerized.

At first I don't see anything, but finally I make out two shadowy figures at the dig. Judging by size, one of them has to be Rocky. The other probably is Seth, since that seems to be the only crewmember he has left.

"Does that fool never stop?" Morgan says, and I'm pretty sure he's not asking for my opinion. I'm equally certain I don't want to be in the middle of his latest rage.

Morgan shakes his fist at Rocky's shadowy image. "Go on, fool. Work till you drop. If you think you can stop me from grabbing the jade treasures and the headlines, you're dumber than you look."

He snarls at the monitors, then storms toward

the back room muttering, "We'll see how interested he is in working all night after I turn loose my secret weapon."

Secret weapon? What fresh horror is that? I picture a couple of hungry crocodiles chained in a pit somewhere out back, waiting to be turned loose for the meal Morgan has deprived them of since last Tuesday. I've just lost all interest in the cute Bernardo alligator-skin sandals I've been hoping make it to the after-Thanksgiving shoe sale.

Thinking of the alligators and a whole class of shoes now fallen into disfavor, I'm almost too upset to use my hairpin.

In the other room, Morgan is moving around, slamming cabinet doors, and rattling dishes. Within minutes, I smell coffee.

With nothing in my stomach but a meager breakfast and a few crumbs of bread, I'd do just about anything for a cup of coffee. In my current circumstances, I have about as much chance of getting one as I do of winning Mooreville Elementary PTO's "Mother of the Year" award next spring.

Movement on one of the monitors catches my eye. It's Juanita hurrying out of the guest cottage. What's she doing there at this time of night? Getting more sheets for Morgan's ghostly invasions of Tulum? Or does she plan to do some haunting herself?

Outside the cottage, she bumps into Mama and Fayrene, still in costume. All three women scream.

"Question her, Mama. Find out what she's doing there."

I make no pretense of being quiet. I've already sassed old man Morgan and kicked him where it hurts most. No need to start acting meek at this late date. He'd never believe it.

Figuring I don't have much to lose, I yell at him, "I could use a cup of coffee in here." No response. What did I expect?

On the monitors, Mama and Fayrene go inside the cottage, congratulating each other on the success of their latest native ceremony.

"That ghost won't dare set his foot in Tulum again," Mama says.

"Just think, Ruby Nell. We can have inner animal ceremonies in our new séance room at Gas, Grits, and Guts."

"I can see what a hit that would be with Jarvetis."

So can I. If it weren't for Jarvetis' upright Baptist reputation and Uncle Charlie's intervention, Mama and Fayrene would already be the talk of Mooreville with their Friday afternoons in the back room at Gas, Grits, and Guts—gambling plus sweet tea laced with whatever spirits they happen to have. I'm not sure they could quell the gossip if the two of them go native.

"Watching a little TV?" To my surprise, old

man Morgan appears in the doorway in a jovial mood. He's also carrying two cups of coffee. I guess thinking about his secret weapon has improved his spirits. Either that or he's put poison in my cup.

Holding one of them just out of my reach, he tells me, "Say please."

"In your dreams."

"I never figured you for the feisty kind." He waves the coffee under my nose, and I nearly pass out from caffeine desire. "If you're thinking I've put something in it, you're wrong. We're not through with you yet."

To my great surprise, he hands over a cup of steaming coffee that smells and tastes like Starbucks. When you live alone, one of the few pleasures you have is great coffee, so you learn to make the best.

Maybe there's enough of the human left in Morgan that given half a chance and a few years of intense therapy, he can turn over a new leaf. Listen, call me sappy, but I'm a great believer in second chances. For other people, that is.

Or is this new line of thinking a sign that my captor is winning me over to his side? That a subtle brainwashing is taking place that will steal whatever it is that makes me Callie Valentine Jones and send me away—if I ever *get* away—as somebody in the same body but with a whole 'nother set of sensibilities?

To steel myself against such a possibility, I conjure up the horrors that Morgan has put me through. Let alone Lovie and Elvis.

While he straddles a chair a few feet from me, facing the monitors, I shore up my defenses and savor the brew.

"Keep digging, you fool," he says to the monitor showing Rocky slaving away at his dig. Then he turns to face me.

"I knew that redheaded cousin of yours would be a wildcat from the get-go. But you've surprised me. I guess you got it from your mama. Danged if she didn't nearly expose me as the ghost tonight."

"Too bad she didn't." I lift the coffee cup. "Your hospitality notwithstanding, I'm ready to leave."

"It's not happening unless you're Houdini."

"What do you plan to do with me? Kill me like you did your wife?"

"Who said I killed her?"

"What happened?"

"Wouldn't you like to know?"

Morgan enjoys playing cat-and-mouse games. Listen, when it comes to reading people, I'll put a hairstylist up against a psychologist any day.

"Oh, I'll know, all right. With Jack on the cold case, it won't be long before the entire world knows."

"Cold case, my left foot. He left on a wild goose chase in Cozumel."

I get this sinking feeling that I hope doesn't show.

"Jack's on the island?"

"Yep. My partners planted stuff from your purse all over the island. That ought to keep him out of my hair for a while."

I picture myself withering away in this shack for years, finally emerging like somebody from a time capsule, aged and changed so much that no one knows me.

"Jack won't be fooled for long. He'll be back."

"Maybe I'll ship him a little present." He walks over, grabs my left hand, and inspects the engagement and wedding rings I should have taken off long ago but didn't; don't ask me why.

"What do you think? Should I get Miss Ruby Nell and Mrs. Johnson back to the island and make them disappear, or should I send Jack a little present from you? Maybe this finger? You think he'd recognize the rings?"

I hold back the scream building in my throat. Haven't I read the best defense is a tough offense? Briefly, I consider dumping my hot coffee over Morgan.

"Is that what you did with your wife? Chopped her into little pieces?"

Something registers on Morgan's face, but I can't make out what it is. Fear does that, steals judgment.

Morgan flings my left hand away, then stomps back to his chair.

"I didn't kill Lucille. I loved her."

I'm a good listener, a soft touch, and a sucker for a love story. Even if I weren't the best hairstylist in the state, my compassion alone would make me the most popular woman in Mooreville. Listen, that's why women flock to Hair.Net even when they don't have appointments. They love to hang around on my pink vinyl seats and share their latest domestic bliss or troubles, whichever the case may be. If it's the latter, the Prohibition Punch is only a few feet away.

I wish I had some now. I'd ply old man Morgan with Lovie's recipe and we'd cry together. Maybe I could pull off a miracle and he'd have a change of heart. Then we'd hug and promise to send Christmas cards before I waltzed out of here a free woman.

"Your wife's disappearance must have devastated you."

"She didn't disappear."

"What happened?"

"We got into a spat that got out of hand. We were tussling, I guess I shoved her a little too hard, and she fell down the Jade goddess' temple steps."

My sudden sympathy takes a powder. "If it was an accident, why did you report her missing?"

195

"Use your brain, girlie. A Mexican prison is not the place you'd want to spend the rest of your life. I covered it all up."

I don't ask how. I don't even watch the grisly scenes in scary movies; I put my hands over my eyes.

In danger of becoming an accident victim myself, or at least of losing a digit, especially with Jack on a wild goose chase in Cozumel, I don't want to know what Morgan is capable of.

But what if he's lying? About everything. He's done it before.

Determined not to let my worries get the best of me, I discreetly study him while we both finish our coffee. He's the same sly, untrustworthy-looking old man who set my teeth on edge when I first met him. A casting director's dream if you're looking for someone to fill the role of the perfect ax murderer. It's all in his eyes. They're hard, beady, and shifty.

My captor looks fully capable of cutting off one of my body parts and sending it to Jack in a box. If I don't want to lose my ring finger—or worse—I'd better put some magic on my hairpin.

Finally Morgan yawns and stretches. Then he gets out of his chair and rocks back on his heels. A sign of cockiness. A sure signal he's planning to say something that will give me nightmares.

"Maybe I'll send a foot instead of a finger." Morgan's statement ratchets up my stress level a hundred percent. "Give it some thought tonight, girlie. You can let me know in the morning."

How did he know that one of my greatest simple pleasures is wearing designer shoes? The idea of one shoe and a peg leg takes all the glamour out of cute shoes.

With his latest zinger reducing me to a woman holding back hysteria, Morgan heads toward the back of the shack, where I assume he has another bed as flimsy and filthy as this one. I hope it's filled with tarantulas with a taste for mean old men's tough feet. Maybe then Morgan won't be so eager to deprive me of one of mine.

For a while I hear him moving around back there. As soon as all movement stops, I retrieve my loose hairpin from under my left hip and set to work as if I have only hours left with my very own feet.

Which could just turn out to be the awful truth.

Elvis' Opinion #12 on Jungle Fauna, Bad Booze, and Burnin' Love

Neck deep in jungle flora, I decide it's time to hotfoot back to the village. I just hope I don't encounter any jungle fauna. My basset suit's not sequined, but I'm partial to it. I don't hanker to get it mauled by sharp teeth and sullied with poisoned fangs.

"Any Day Now" is my escape mantra as well

as my song du jour. By the time I've howled one verse, I'm back at the village and scuttling into the hut to see what fresh hell awaits.

Sure enough, Lovie is stuffing herself with something that looks like fried dried flowers and quaffing bad booze like there's no tomorrow. Which there won't be if I don't get her sober enough to shag her national treasure out of here.

Doing my best "Tiger Man" performance, I barrel across the mean hut and knock her cup to the ground. She says a word that would make hardened criminals quake. I kindly remind her that "True Love Travels on a Gravel Road."

Some call it tough love.

Listen, I've got news for Lovie. I'll knock over every drink the natives bring in here. If we're going to survive a jungle escape, it's going to take both of us with our fully functioning wits.

Unfortunately, Lovie doesn't get the picture. She lurches from her makeshift throne and staggers toward the door muttering, "I'm parched." If she gets outside, floundering around in the dark in her condition, there's no telling what will happen.

I beat her to the door, plant my ample self in her way and reveal my plans by humming a few bars of "It's Nice to Go Traveling."

"Move, dog."

Obviously, she did not get the hint.

Even worse, calling me *dog* is an insult

tantamount to calling me a Lhasa apso. Listen, Lovie loves me like a brother. She's never insulted me. Which just goes to show her advanced state of inebriation.

I try nudging her back inside, which ought to get me nominated as Brave Dog of the Year. Lovie's no small person. A hundred ninety pounds of "Good Rockin' Tonight," to hear her tell it. It takes courage to risk getting flattened by that "Hunk'a Burnin' Love."

She tries to finesse her way out through an opening on the left. But finesse and booze are incompatible. She topples and I barely escape with my swivel intact.

I sniff my way around her prone body to see if there's any damage. Let me tell you, my nose is a better diagnostician than some vets I know (who shall remain nameless). I'm a dog of principle.

Satisfied Lovie went down limp and didn't break bones or tear cartilage, I lie down and cuddle up beside her. I'm beat. And, as Miss Scarlett would say, "Tomorrow is another day."

Listen, I'm a dog of letters. I've read the book. What Southerner worth his salt hasn't? (Or at least seen the movie.)

Speaking of which . . . I doze off dreaming of *Love Me Tender*, which is not only one of my many box office smashes in Tinseltown, plus a smash hit single, but also my modus operandi with my foxy French poodle.

Chapter 16

Hairpins, Secret Partners, and Kinky Moves

Spurred by visions of myself with only one foot while Lovie and Elvis are lost forever in the jungle, I work in the dark with Rocky to keep me company. Not in person, of course. On the monitors, his cohort at his side, digging to find the lost tomb of the Nine Lords. And apparently a bunch of jade treasures, to boot.

Pushing my hairpin into the lock, I whisper, *Come on, come on.* I guess I'm praying for a miracle. The pin shoots out of my left hand and lands beyond the reach of my restraints. To my overwrought ears, it sounds like a cat being thrown against the wall.

I hold my breath, but all I hear from Morgan's room is the sound of snorting, hissing snores. Pulling another hairpin from my bedraggled French twist, I tackle the lock with renewed vigor.

Since the universe seems to be fresh out of miracles, I'm on my own.

Or maybe *come on* is not the right prayer when you're scheduled for dismemberment in an ancient Mayan ruin. "Please, please," I whisper.

The pin slides into the lock, then meets

resistance, bends sharply, and shoots toward the ceiling.

I will not cry. Until I get safely back to Mooreville. And then I might start bawling and never stop.

A faint band of light seeping around the thick shutters on the window tells me it's almost morning.

Soon Morgan will come in here with a sharp knife to cut off my finger. Or my foot. Who knows what body part he'll think of next?

I'm down to my last hope and my last hairpin. When I pull it from my French twist, my hair tumbles around my face in tangles. I feel sour and sweaty.

If my clients could see me now, I'd be out of a job. I pride myself on being my own best advertisement.

Of the many indignities of being a captive, one of the most insidious is not being able to maintain even minimum hygiene and beauty. I wonder about the state poor Lovie must be in, being held for days in the jungle.

Saying a little prayer for Lovie and Elvis, I insert my lone remaining means of escape into the lock at my right wrist. For a breathless moment, I feel resistance, then a slight twist, an indrawn breath . . . and the handcuff swings open. I catch it before it falls to the floor and wakes old man Morgan. Now that I have the hang of it, I use one quick flick of the wrist to jimmy the lock on my leg irons.

And I am free!

The front door is about five feet away. I'm there in seconds, moving quietly, holding my breath. Alas, it's a deadbolt, requiring a key.

Guess who has it.

The only other means of escape is the window, and it's shuttered and nailed down. I refuse to be daunted. I'll simply have to overpower old man Morgan, take his keys, and let myself out. And I'm not about to scare myself into timidity by dwelling on my earlier failure to secure the keys.

I stuff the hairpin into my pocket and tiptoe around the room, searching for anything I can use as a weapon. I could club him with the bed if I were seven feet tall and bench-pressed Texas for fun. Or I could hide in the closet and fell him with a bull's-eye hit with one of the two mothballs I see on the floor. Alternatively, I might throw the "hopeful" wool coat over his head and smother him into submission. (I say *hopeful* because why would you keep a wool coat in the jungle unless you hoped to someday leave the heat and snakes and crocodiles behind and end up in New York watching Macy's Thanksgiving Day Parade?)

The only possible weapons in this room are the monitors on the wall and Morgan's straight-backed chair.

I sink into the chair, and my empty stomach gives such a vigorous protest it's a wonder I don't wake the Mayan mummies.

"Well, look'a here."

Holy cow! Morgan is standing in the doorway leering at me. The only good thing I can say is he's carrying neither gun nor cutlery.

The bad thing is that while I'm sitting here in shock, he's heading my way.

I leap up, grab the chair, and swing. The brunt of the blow lands with a satisfying *thwack* in his groin. Morgan goes down on his knees, clutching himself, screaming.

Taking aim, I bring the chair down onto the back of his head. Still scrambling on the floor, he yells words that would shock even Lovie.

Why won't this man go down? I leap onto his back and grab him by the hair.

"Hand over the keys or lose body parts."

"How do you plan to do that, girlie?"

He tries to buck me off, but I hang on. Listen, he's dealing with a farm girl. In my youth, I rode my share of horses and even bucking yearling calves.

I whip my hairpin out of my pocket and press the tip against Morgan's throat.

"Do you want me to give you a new windpipe first or would you rather lose an eyeball?"

With a horrific crash the door is kicked from its hinges and Jack Jones roars into the room.

Relieved doesn't begin to cover my feelings. All I can say is somebody ought to name a building after him. Maybe even a whole town.

Bleary-eyed, disheveled, and dangerously coiled, he looks more demon than human. I wouldn't want to be Morgan.

"Kinky, Callie. Now, move back."

I'll argue later. For now, common sense takes precedence over independence. I jump off Morgan's back and out of Jack's way. Before Morgan can get off all fours, Jack jerks him up and dangles him in the air.

"Did he touch you, Cal?"

"No."

"This is your lucky day, Morgan."

With that, Jack knocks him senseless, then cuffs him to the bed with the shackles I no longer need.

"Get the key," I yell, but Jack's half a step ahead of me.

If I were a vindictive and violent woman, I'd march over there and kick old man Morgan. As it is I feel sorry for him. By the time he serves his sentence in Mexico for covering up his wife's death and kidnapping two U.S. citizens, not to mention my dog, he'll wish he was resting peacefully in the fabled tomb of the Nine Lords.

"You okay, Cal?" I nod, and Jack pulls out his cell phone.

While he gives Uncle Charlie a quick recap, I

race through the caretaker's shack looking for my own cell phone. I find it on Morgan's bedside table.

Snatching it up, I march back to the front room where Jack drapes his arm around me and leads me to the door.

"Let's get you out of here. You look like death warmed over. It's a good thing I got here when I did."

"If you'll care to remember, I had already rescued myself."

I'll think about the sins of pride later. Right now, I just can't let my almost-ex think I can't make it without him.

"I would never underestimate a stylist with a hairpin."

His chuckle spoils the compliment. If he even meant it as one in the first place.

"Jack Jones, the minute we get stateside, I want divorce papers signed."

"Yes ma'am. It's at the top of my list. After we find Lovie."

Good grief, I ought to be ashamed, talking divorce with my cousin missing. I blame an empty stomach and unwashed hair.

"Morgan admitted he took her," I tell Jack. "He has partners. At least two of them."

"Do you know who they are?"

"No. I think one is female." I tell him my suspicions about the Farkles, then Juanita and

Rosita, leaving out a few details. Like how I went snooping. "We've got to find Lovie and Elvis fast before the other kidnappers panic over Morgan's capture and do something horrible."

"How did you happen to come up with that particular set of suspects?" This is not an idle question. Those aren't in Jack's vocabulary.

The guest cottage is just ahead. If I wait long enough to answer Jack, maybe Mama or Uncle Charlie will rush out to greet me and Jack will forget about putting me in the hot seat.

But I pride myself on being a thrifty, independent woman. If you don't count shoes. And all that dog and cat food I have to buy for Elvis and my rescues.

Oh, well. "Would you believe the ceremony of the jade-green skirts?"

"We'll discuss skirts later. Right now, let's get you fed and bathed."

"I'll take care of that all by myself, thank you very much. And you leave my skirts out of this. You have better things to do."

Mama and Fayrene are the first to spot us. Screaming, "My baby!" Mama lifts the hem of her hibiscus pink caftan, races my way, and nearly bowls me over with a hug.

Fayrene is not far behind. Both are clinging to me as if I've been gone for years. Over the top of their heads I see Jack watching me.

"Cal, I have urgent things to do. But nothing better." He winks, then strolls off.

"What was that all about?" Leave it to Mama. Where Jack's and my private business is concerned, she never misses a beat.

"Mama, can I bathe and eat first? I'm grungy and I'm starving."

Chapter 17

Bad Blood, Bat Blood, and True Blood

It's not until I'm safely back inside the guest cottage that I notice both Mama and Fayrene are wearing feathers in their hair.

"Mama, what in the world? Are you going native?"

"Shhh. I don't want Charlie to hear."

While we are in the kitchen Uncle Charlie is somewhere down the hall, casing and debugging the joint, as Lovie would say.

"Don't you think he's already noticed? Holy cow, Mama, you're wearing buzzard feathers."

"These are erotic feathers," Fayrene chimes in.

"For Lovie?"

"No, for you," Fayrene says. Mama tries to shush her, but she keeps on prattling. "If we can find the blood of a bat, we're going to do a reunion ceremony."

If I were "at myself," as Fayrene would say, I'd try to talk them out of another ceremony. So far, their native rituals have produced nothing but disaster. That I am grateful just goes to show the subtle shifts that take place in the psyche when you're kidnapped. Even if it's for only a short while.

I shudder to think about the Lovie and the Elvis I'll be getting back.

Uncle Charlie comes into the kitchen and puts his arm around me. "Take your time getting cleaned up and changed. When you show up for breakfast, act natural and don't mention a thing about Morgan. I want to see some unguarded reactions."

Uncle Charlie explains the situation in great detail, and I'm glad. If I had my choice, I wouldn't want my fate—and Lovie's—hanging on the chance that these two would keep their mouths shut.

And I mean that in the best of ways. I love Mama and Fayrene, but the mambo murders in Memphis proved my point. Enough said.

"Where's Jack?" I ask.

"He and Rocky are making sure the Mexican authorities find out where Morgan has hidden Lovie." Uncle Charlie kisses my cheek. "Take your time, dear heart. You've been through a lot."

After he leaves, Mama says, "For Pete's sake,

Fayrene, I told Charlie my feathers were a frivolous fashion accessory. I thought I was going to have to muzzle you."

"You and which army?"

Oh, Lord. "I need a bath."

Mama and Fayrene follow me to the bathroom, then stand guard outside the door. Though I protest that I can do this myself, I don't need bodyguards, I have to say this is one time I'm glad Mama doesn't listen to me. I'm feeling so skittish I don't want to be anywhere alone.

How that's going to translate when I get ready for bed and Jack's across the hall (I hope), I don't even want to think about.

There's a tap on the door. "You all right in there?" Mama calls.

"I'm fine." This is only partially true. I still feel like I'm back at the shack worrying about walking with a peg leg and dreaming about taking a bath. I worry I might wake up any minute and it will be Morgan outside my door.

While I turn on the water, step into the tub, and soak myself, I can hear Mama and Fayrene outside the door arguing about who said what and the best place to obtain the blood of a bat.

Though I'm certain Uncle Charlie was thorough in his search, I glance around for unwanted visitors. I don't trust snakes. The two-legged kind or any other kind. You never know. One could be lurking to bite off the body parts still intact thanks to old man Morgan's unfortunate morning.

Another tap on the door. "Cal, it's Mama. Are you okay?"

I don't tell her this is the fifth time she's asked. I'm just grateful. "Yes," I say, then consider myself lucky to have family and friends who care. When I get Elvis and Lovie back, I'm going to make a long list of all the reasons I have to be thankful.

I guess I can start by being grateful I'm alive. Even so, after I patch my scrapes and scratches with ointment and Band-Aids, I look like the unfortunate Bride of Frankenstein.

Mama and Fayrene follow me down the hall and into my bedroom, where Mama proceeds to plop onto my bed and Fayrene proceeds to search my closet.

"Do you mind?" I tell them. "I'd like to get dressed."

"I've seen it all," Mama says. "Who do you think changed your diapers? Fairies?"

Deep in the bowels of my closet, Fayrene says, "You can never take anything for granite, Callie. There's no telling who could be hiding in here."

I give up. And I confess—I'm secretly pleased.

"Since you're already in my closet, toss me out some clothes. I'd like to eat breakfast in something besides a bath towel."

Fayrene emerges with a pair of blue-jean shorts

and a white tee shirt, then joins Mama on my bed. I would have chosen a perkier color— probably yellow—but at least this one matches my bandages.

After I dress, the three of us head toward the main cottage, just in time for breakfast.

"Mama, remember what Uncle Charlie told us. Fayrene, you, too."

"For Pete's sake, Carolina, we have sense enough to keep our mouths shut."

"Don't worry about me. I understand the elephant of surprise."

For once, Fayrene got it right. If there were ever a moment when the element of surprise could become an elephant, this would be it. Everybody at the dig knows I've been missing. The question is, who wanted me to vanish and who will be upset by my sudden reappearance?

Now that Morgan's been turned over to the authorities, the cold case is solved. But there are still at least two people hanging around Tulum who will do anything to sabotage Rocky's dig.

Or are they on the island at the undertakers' convention?

With their arms looped around my waist, Mama and Fayrene flank me. I guess they're afraid if they aren't touching me, I'll get carried off by the ghosts of Tulum. Believe me, I have no intention of getting bushwhacked again, by Morgan or anybody else. From now on, I'm keeping hairpins in my pocket and adopting Lovie's *don't mess with me* attitude.

We don't encounter a soul on the path to the main cottage. I find that odd, since Juanita is always around with an armload of sheets. Has she already found out Morgan's been arrested? Is she holed up somewhere with Morgan's other silent partner wondering what their next move will be?

Only two people are in the courtyard when we arrive: Uncle Charlie and Rocky's second-in-command, Seth Alford.

"Good morning." I smile like I'm on a commercial for whitening toothpaste.

Seth looks slightly shell-shocked. Guilt or relief? He recovers quickly and comes running over to sweep me into a tight hug.

"Callie, I'm so glad to see you. We were frantic looking for you."

I ease out of his grip. He's treating me like a long-lost favorite relative. His reaction not only seems excessive but also makes me uncomfortable.

Listen, I know Lovie and I are warm and friendly, prone to quick hugs and air kisses with people we've just met while reapplying passion pink lipstick in a public bathroom, but I've never been in a public bathroom with Seth Alford.

Of course, he did have breakfast with me while I was wearing baby doll pajamas. That sort of thing could cause a false sense of intimacy. Besides, I can't picture this bright, open-faced young man as anything but sincere.

Lovie says I rationalize too much. Based on that first look on Seth's face, she'd be ready to march him off and throttle him with her baseball bat. Or sit on him till he squealed the truth. The poor young man she flattened in Las Vegas during the Bubbles Caper probably still can't catch a painless breath.

Grabbing my plate, I walk to the buffet, where Mama and Fayrene close ranks again. I wonder how long it will take before Mama loses interest in being my watchdog and moves on to more exciting pursuits (probably involving war paint and feathers or a hefty chunk from my bank account).

There's not as much food as usual on the table. Does that mean Rosita knew I was in the caretaker's cottage and wouldn't be here for breakfast?

Of course, slim pickings at breakfast are not enough to make her a suspect. With Jack and Uncle Charlie turning this place upside down, plus Mama and Fayrene doing no-telling-what-all, everybody on staff knew I was missing. Including the cook.

I take two of everything and pour myself a huge glass of orange juice, and then head back to the table.

"Where's Rosita?" Uncle Charlie and I seem to be thinking along the same lines.

"I'll check on her," Seth says. "She needs to be out here hustling things along so we can start searching for Lovie."

He rushes off, and Mama pulls out her Hollywood cigarette holder, a sign somebody's in big trouble. I'm just glad it's not me.

"What was that all about, Charlie?"

"Jack called before you got here. Morgan denies having partners and claims to know nothing of Lovie's whereabouts."

"But he confessed to me, Uncle Charlie. He talked about his partners."

"It's your word against his, dear heart, and he knows that."

"They believed that lying rat, didn't they, Charlie?" Mama's blowing smoke rings, now, and her feathers are quivering. Not a good sign. Listen, smoke rings mean there's bad blood between Mama and somebody. Currently, that somebody would be Archie Morgan.

"I'm afraid the authorities did, Ruby Nell."

"You get out there and take Morgan down. Make him talk, Charlie. Nobody messes with a Valentine and gets away with it."

Elvis' Opinion #13 on Babies, Names, and Destiny

Lovie's groaning brings me out of doggie dreamland. She sits up, holding her head. "Where in the devil am I?"

I'm so happy to see her coming back around, I cut loose with a little "Welcome to My World."

"Elvis?" She gives me a bleary-eyed look, then proceeds to inspect herself, feathers, war paint, and all. "What is this shit? I look like a molting turkey."

Doesn't she remember? I do a clever rendition of "Too Much Monkey Business," which turns out to be brilliant thinking on my part. Lovie shakes herself all over, clearing out the cobwebs, and then she rises to her feet, all magnificent hundred ninety pounds of her.

Outside our hut, the natives are stirring. Lovie watches them awhile, trying to get the lay of the land, then she stomps over and sits on her throne.

"If they'd meant to kill us, they'd have already done it. What do you think, boy?"

She may look a bit shaky on her feet, but at least she's no longer calling me *dog*. I take that as a very good sign.

I march over to my pottery bowls and nose them around to show Lovie I've been well-fed. Then I do a swivel-hipped version of "Treat Me Nice."

Lovie's smart. She gets the picture. Inspecting her paint and feathers again, she begins to chuckle. The only sound I can think of more wonderful than Lovie's full-blown laughter is my sweet Frenchie in the throes of heat.

"Looks like the natives are treating us like gods. Well, much as I appreciate being a goddess, I'm fixing to get the heck out of Dodge."

Lovie goes from laughter to flinty-eyed determination. If you've never seen a steel magnolia on the warpath, you've missed one of the world's greatest wonders.

"We're getting out of here tonight, Elvis. I've got some unfinished business in Tulum."

Lovie's my kind of gal. Trouble is her middle name and kicking some serious butt is her game. This is one show I don't want to miss.

All I can say is the kidnapper doesn't stand a chance.

Suddenly my nose starts twitching and my mismatched ears pick up sounds. I scurry outside just in time to catch a glimpse of somebody disappearing around the side of the hut. A woman, it looks like. Was it the old woman who speaks English? Did she overhear our escape plans?

I don't have time to ponder because another parade of pregnant native girls is heading our way. I hurry back inside and give Lovie a heads-up by howling a few bars of "This Is Our Dance."

Quick on the draw, Lovie slouches in her makeshift throne and relaxes her face so she appears to be in a glassy-eyed stupor.

The giggling gaggle of girls come inside and approach her, offering a cup of native brew, all chattering at once.

A lesser dog would get caught up in their party mood, but a dog with mismatched ears for trouble and a keen detective mind, to boot, is not about to lose sight of the fact that we're in the midst of the enemy.

My finely tuned instincts are confirmed when I feel a shadow fall over me. I glance up to see the one-and-only English-speaking woman gliding into the hut. Tightlipped and silent, she's as impassive as the shell of an English walnut. But let me tell you, I don't read faces—I read auras. And hers is black as the tar Tinseltown reviewers use on entertainers who can't sing.

I try to warn Lovie, but she's too busy being a goddess to notice.

She waves the cup away, and then surprises the heck out of the natives by lifting her hands and saying, "State your wishes. I am the goddess of the sun, the moon, the stars. I am the goddess of all things fertile and good."

She sounds so ethereal and goddess-like, she nearly fools me.

Still expressionless, the old woman interprets, and the girls fall onto their knees in front of Lovie's throne. Some of them even kiss her feet.

Well, bless'a my soul. From the looks of things, it wouldn't take much more of this adulation to win Lovie over to the notion that she could be a Mayan goddess forever. When we get home I'll have to have a heart-to-howl chat with her about the pitfalls of being a celebrity.

In the background, I try some serious body language to tell her to *suck it up and pull out of it. Listen, Dorothy, we're no longer in Kansas.*

Finally Lovie pulls herself together. "Rise," she intones, and one by one the native girls stand up to present their big bare bellies to her.

"Tell baby sex and name," the old woman commands. "Bestow blessing."

Lovie never misses a beat. She puts her hand on the first belly and acts like she's vanished into the netherworld of wise goddess gurus. If she had my talent and savoir faire, she'd throw in a little hip swiveling and some well-placed sneers.

"Boy," she intones. "His name is Stalking Panther. He will have the strength of warriors."

To the next two, she says, "Girl, her name is Dancing Moon. Great beauty is her gift." And then, "Boy, his name is Tall Trees. He will be filled with wisdom and courage."

It's all I can do to keep from rolling around on

my mat laughing. From her throne, Lovie steamrolls ahead.

"Boy, his name is Wide Waters. He's deep as the sea, smart and bright. Girl, her name is Yellow Bird. She will run so fast it seems she's flying."

My human mom says Lovie always got the lead in school plays, and every Halloween, Fayrene sets her up in the back room at Gas, Grits, and Guts with a gypsy costume and a crystal ball. It wouldn't be Halloween in Mooreville without Lovie telling fortunes.

Trey, Jarvetis' best redbone hound and my best friend, says they sell more pickled pigs' lips on Allhallows Eve than any other time of the year. He credits Lovie.

I sit on my royal haunches and enjoy the rest of Lovie's show. She seems so good at divining the sex of unborn babies, even I start to wonder if she has a gift.

Listen, never underestimate the link between a child's name and his destiny. Take me, for instance. Mention my given name, and everybody in the world knows you're talking about a King.

Maybe when my sweet Frenchie comes around again, I'll take her to Lovie to find out if we're going to get lucky and have three handsome basset boys instead of only one, like we did last time.

Ann-Margret's human mom is calling the boy Spot, of all the insulting things. I'd have gone with DJ in honor of DJ Fontana, one of my best backups ever. Plus, DJ has a nice strong ring to it.

I've told Ann-Margret I don't care what they call him, no son of mine is going to be named Spot. It sounds like something spilled on a rug that you'd want to spray with Woolite.

Over by Lovie's throne the pregnant girls are grooming Lovie's hair, festooning it with flowers. This could go on all day.

I glance around to see what the old woman is up to, but she has vanished. This can't be good. My dog detective instincts tell me she didn't go outside to sing "Queenie Wahine's Papaya."

Feigning innocence, I stretch my ample self like I'm doing a little doggie calisthenics, and then I mosey on out of the hut.

Usually an appearance by the long lipped god spurs a rush of admirers who follow me around imitating my every move. Today, my fans are in clusters around the perimeter of the village, and they're busier than that silly cocker spaniel when he's digging up the whole back yard trying to find my hidden stash of ham bones.

This calls for some skullduggery. I suck in my portly gut and slink from tree to tree, my ears on radar and my nose to the ground.

I smell "T-R-O-U-B-L-E." These natives are

swinging ropes and nets from every tree in the area, and they're not building a "Mansion Over the Hilltop."

What they're building are traps.

A lesser dog would be trembling in his hind legs. But it would be a mistake to underestimate me. I continue to suck up my gut, go into *Kid Galahad* mode, prance into the middle of the village square, and howl a few bars of "King of the Whole Wide World."

Listen, I'm a dog of valor. Act like a scaredy-cat and you end up eating Meow Mix.

Chapter 18

Feathers, Ceremonies, and Elvis Sightings

I know Uncle Charlie well enough to be certain he won't take Mama's radical path and beat the truth out of old man Morgan. But the strain of the futile search for Lovie is beginning to show. For one thing, he hasn't shaved, and for another, he hasn't quoted a single line of Shakespeare.

Always when the family is frazzled and threatening to come apart at the seams, Uncle Charlie comes up with some pithy Shakespearean quote that makes us all feel better. Don't ask me why. Maybe it's the way he speaks, ever confident and hopeful.

My kidnapping only added to his strain. I've got to be more careful. And smarter.

Think, I tell myself. Surely there's something I'm missing, some small detail about my kidnapping that would solve this case if only I could remember it.

Suddenly Mama says, "I wonder what's keeping Seth?"

"My ESPN tells me he's up to no good."

Fayrene could be onto something. After all, he's the only man left in Rocky's crew. Why didn't he spook and run? Is he hanging around out of loyalty to Rocky or loyalty to old man Morgan? And if so, why? What's Seth's connection to Morgan? And to Rosita?

Fayrene's right. Something's up in the kitchen.

The thought of sneaking back there to find out gives me the shivers. What if one or both were involved in my kidnapping? What if they're plotting my recapture right this very minute? Or worse, my murder.

I'm dithering between sleuthing or playing it safe when the matter is taken completely out of my hands.

"Jack!" Mama rushes toward him as if a fatted calf killed in honor of his return is roasting on the spit.

Rocky's with him, his face drawn and his fists clenching and unclenching.

"I wanted to beat the truth out of Morgan,"

Rocky says. "If Jack hadn't stopped me, I'd have killed him."

"The authorities should have turned Jack loose on him," Mama says. "He'd get at the truth." She thinks my almost-ex can turn water to wine.

"I've already spent a little *quality time* with Morgan, Ruby Nell. He's not talking."

You can bet Morgan's "quality time" with Jack Jones a.k.a. the Black Panther was not something you'd want to talk about with your grandchildren over Christmas dinner. If The Company's most lethal operative can't get the truth out of Morgan, nobody can.

Jack fills his plate at the buffet, comes back to the table, and assesses me like I'm his favorite strawberry jam and he's fixing to spread me all over his hot toast.

I thought I was half-dead till he looked at me like that. Leave it to Jack to prove me wrong.

He winks, then sits down in the chair next to mine and proceeds to attack his food. Jack eats the way he does everything else, with energy and apparent single-minded concentration.

I say *apparent* because what you see with Jack is not what you get. There's nothing single-minded about him. A peek into his multitasking, steel-trap, formidable brain would probably scare the average person to death.

Uncle Charlie and Rocky ease over to the coffeepot, settling for only dark, sugarless brew.

If this were a movie, they'd be cast in rolls of the serious but fatherly cop and the grieving young lover.

When Rocky comes to the table, I watch something deep in Jack unfold. From the look in his eyes, I'd say he's not fixing to deliver a Christmas package.

"Rocky, what do you know about Seth Alford?"

"He's a good archeologist. Well credentialed and fully capable to take over when I'm not at the dig."

"Why would a young, bright archeologist take a back seat and watch you get credit for a historic discovery?"

Rocky takes off his hat and puts it on his knee. Trying to center himself, it looks like. The hatband is already damp with sweat and has left an indentation in his hair.

I wish Lovie could see this. I think she'd find it endearing.

"What are you getting at, Jones?"

Looks like Jack has met his match. If the Valentine family weren't in such dire straits, I'd giggle.

"Your second-in-command keeps trying to take charge of the search for Lovie."

Rocky stands up, a big, intimidating man. Anybody but Jack might think twice about crossing him. "Are you implying something, Jones?"

"Just pointing out the facts."

"Seth's crazy about her. Everybody is. Lovie's like that. People are drawn to her. Besides, I want him in charge."

I wonder if anybody else sees the look that passes between Jack and Uncle Charlie. Probably. But I'm the only one here who knows its significance—two Company men, one former, one current, telepathizing that Seth Alford warrants further investigation.

But if he were my kidnapper, wouldn't I have recognized something about him? His size, his voice, his scent, for goodness' sake. If you pay attention, you can tell one male from another simply by scent.

As the seed of doubt Jack planted begins to sink in, Rocky looks like a man trying to get his bearings.

"Seth knows this jungle better than I do." Rocky sounds as if he's trying to convince himself.

"Why?" This from Uncle Charlie.

"Did I hear someone call my name?" Seth strolls back onto the patio, carrying a map, looking as innocent as the little boy who always gets picked to play a cherub in the Christmas pageant. He plucks an apple turnover from a plate, then straddles a chair. "All's well in the kitchen. What do you want me to do today, boss? Search for Miss Lovie while you work at the dig?"

"Forget the lost tomb of the Nine Lords." Rocky rams his hat back on his head. "We've got to find Lovie."

"I knew that's what you'd say." Seth spreads a map over the table. "I've laid out a search pattern."

Given Jack's recent questions regarding Seth's role in the search, you might expect him to leap up and snatch the map out of Seth's hands. But leaping is not in Jack's nature. To the unpracticed eye, he looks like he's just sitting there taking it all in. Uncle Charlie and I know otherwise. He's a man holding a keg of dynamite, just waiting for the right moment to light the fuse.

Seth points to quadrants on the map that show the areas already searched highlighted with yellow, and the vast majority of the map blanketed in pink—unexplored territory.

And somewhere out there are Elvis and Lovie.

The vast pink area gets to me. I have a hard time keeping myself from breaking down and weeping into my rapidly cooling coffee. This won't do. I pull myself together by thinking about the revenge I'm going to take on Morgan's partners.

If I ever find out their identities. Make that, *when*. This is Lovie we're talking about. If I were the one missing in the jungle, she'd be tearing through the trees armed with a baseball bat and no-telling-what-all till she found me.

"Rocky, you and I will take this section." Seth points to an area of pink west of the compound. "Charlie, you and Jack search here." His finger moves to a spot north.

Uncle Charlie nods, and if you didn't know him, you'd think he was agreeing to everything Seth Alford said.

On the other hand, who knows what Jack's thinking? He might as well be an oak tree for all the good it does to try to figure him out.

"Thanks, Seth," Uncle Charlie says, and Rocky gives him a skeptical look.

Poor guy. He's got a lot to learn about the Valentine family.

"That's settled then." Seth folds the map and stuffs it in his pocket. "You ready, Rocky?"

I catch a glimpse of something out the corner of my eye, and quickly turn to see Rosita scuttling back toward the kitchen as if she's been up to no good.

"Did you see her, Uncle Charlie?"

"I did."

"It looked like she was eavesdropping."

"Probably waiting for us to finish so she can clear the dishes."

Suddenly Jack uncoils. "Charlie, take the women back to the hotel on the island. Track Morgan's connections to all suspects."

"What are you going to do, Jack?" I ask.

When he turns to look down at me, I wish I

were standing up. Towering over me while I sit wilted and patched up in my chair, he seems about ten feet tall. And I don't know whether I'm glad about that or mad.

"I'm going to bring Lovie and Elvis back."

"I'm going with you."

"You're going with Charlie."

"She's my cousin and Elvis is my dog."

"The first is true, the second is debatable."

"I'm going, Jack, and that's final."

He gets quiet and I can't tell if he's marshalling further arguments or getting ready to issue commands. When he leans down and puts his hands on my shoulders, gentle-like, tears spring to my eyes. Sometimes, unexpected tenderness unravels me. There is so little of it in this world.

"Cal, I know you would love to go. But you would only slow me down. With one kidnapper caught and the others loose and forewarned, we can't risk losing time."

He's right and I know it. Still, I have my pride. And a stubborn streak, too.

"All right, Jack. You go into that jungle by yourself, but you'd better bring them back."

"I will. I promise."

I lift my chin. I'm not finished yet.

"And don't you dare tell Uncle Charlie to *keep the women safe and out of trouble.* Mama and Fayrene and I have plenty of sense. We're not going to sit in our rooms in Cozumel like three lumps on a log. We're going to help Uncle Charlie get the truth out of the Farkles."

He lets go of my shoulders, all business. "Give her a gun, Charlie. She knows how to use it."

That's stretching things, but I don't let on. Particularly to Jack, who spent hours on the farm trying to teach me to use a firearm.

When he turns on his heels and hurries off, I'm so flabbergasted I can't even move. Who'd have thought? Maybe I impressed him with my hairpin.

"Well, Lord, Callie," Fayrene says. "If you can use a gun, why didn't you get rid of the critters that are eating Ruby Nell's Canadians?"

I think she means caladiums, unless Mama has some foreign men stashed about. Which would be just like her.

I laugh till tears roll down my cheeks. Comic relief will do that to you. A person can take only so much drama. The pressure builds inside, and you have to let it out, one way or the other. The Southern way is laughter through tears.

Within an hour, Fayrene, Mama, Uncle Charlie, and I are all packed and on the ferry heading back to Cozumel. It's a relief to be heading back to civilization, even if we will be in the middle of a bunch of undertakers.

If we can get to the bottom of the Farkle connection, I might even get a chance to slip into the seminar on making up the dead. Not that I need any lessons on makeup for the Glory Land bound. On the contrary, I could teach the rest of them a thing or two.

I'm so good at fixing up the dearly departed at Uncle Charlie's Eternal Rest Funeral Home, I have a stack of requests from my geriatric clients at Hair. Net. The most interesting is from Junie Mae Getty, who drives all the way from Tupelo so I can do her hair.

"Callie, when I go," she told me, "make me up to look like Marilyn Monroe. For once in his life, I want to take the limelight away from Robert Earl."

Robert Earl's the mayor of Tupelo, and his wife Junie Mae stands so far back in his shadow, most folks don't even see her. About the only thing we've ever heard her say in public, is *Hon, it's working,* her way of telling Robert Earl to quit tapping the microphone, it's on.

I promised Junie Mae I'd fix her so even the most diehard fans wouldn't be able to say she wasn't Marilyn, right down to the mole on her left cheek.

Uncle Charlie is standing at the railing between Mama and Fayrene. I wander close enough to catch a drift of the conversation and satisfy myself that no fresh horror is afoot.

He's silent, but Mama and Fayrene are discussing feathers. I don't even want to know.

Leaving them behind, I find a relatively secluded spot on the ferry and call Darlene to check on things at my shop.

The first thing Darlene says is, "Have you found Lovie and Elvis," proving that Mooreville's grapevine is alive and well.

"Not yet, but we're hopeful today will be the day. How are things at Hair.Net?"

"Business is booming," she tells me, which is good news I can use. "Everybody in Mooreville's trying to help Trixie Moffett plan her wedding to Roy Jessup."

"There's no such thing as a private affair in Mooreville."

"I talked Trixie into a blue wedding gown."

"Blue? It's her first wedding."

"Yeah, but her horoscope said she should take a chance and reach for the sky. In my book, that spells blue. Besides, Bobby said Trixie was in danger from white."

"Bobby? Uncle Charlie's assistant?"

"I met him at the funeral home. Claude Akers passed, and he called here asking for you to do the makeup. I went in to pinch-hit."

"Well, thanks." I hope. Listen, I'm a stickler about making the deceased look their very best for the hereafter. I just hope Darlene's work held up to my standards.

"He's a neat guy," Darlene says.

"Who? Akers?"

"No. Bobby."

"Huckabee?"

"Yeah."

Neat is not the word that comes to mind when I think of Bobby. He's clumsy and socially inept and he tries too hard to please. Plus, his psychic blue eye is a bit unsettling.

But I can see how a woman who won't do my clients' nail colors without consulting a horoscope first would be attracted to him. And I'm glad. Really, I am.

"That's great, Darlene," I tell her, and I really mean it. "I'm glad you two are becoming friends."

I pocket my cell phone, then stroll to the railing to join my group. Uncle Charlie is nowhere in sight, and Mama is plucking feathers from her hair, casting them on the water.

"Mama, what's going on?"

"Shhh." Fayrene puts her hands over her lips. "We're doing a *come on home* ceremony."

"Lovie, come back." Mama intones as she casts a shiny black feather toward the sea. It floats over the water awhile and then settles into the waves.

Fayrene chants, "Kumquats, melons, can-ta-loupe."

A few people nearby turn to look at us in a funny way. Which is nothing new. Even in Mooreville, the Valentine entourage attracts attention, which is good both for business and for gossip. I have to say, my family and friends are the backbone of Mooreville's entire social structure.

Another feather flies out of Mama's hand and rises up on a breeze that has sprung up over the Caribbean.

"Oranges, pineapple, man-goes." Fayrene sways while she names off her *erotic* fruits. I can almost hear her thinking how she'll use these so-called native techniques in the back room of Gas, Grits, and Guts.

"We're waiting for you," Mama chants in an ethereal voice, then lets fly another feather. "Come back to us, Elvis."

Nearby, a sixtyish woman in tank top and shorts printed in a purple hibiscus that emphasizes her varicose veins goes into some kind of swoon. An aging man with his shorts' waistband hiked over his large belly by suspenders mops her face with his handkerchief.

"Get away from me, you old fool." The woman shoves him and straightens her tank top. "Elvis is on this boat and I intend to find him."

Chapter 19

Voodoo, Film Noir, and
the Final Journey to Glory Land

When we get off the ferry, we leave behind mild bedlam (nothing new for us) and rumors of Elvis sightings (a more than thirty-year phenomenon that seems to still be going strong).

On the ride to the Cozumel Palace, Mama tries to crank up a discussion of our sleuthing plans, but Uncle Charlie shakes his head and changes the subject.

"The undertakers' convention is probably in full swing," he says.

Mama's smart. She immediately rises to the challenge. "It won't take me long to catch up, Charlie. I'm in a par-tee moood."

"Woo-hoo!" Even Fayrene gets in on the act.

The fact is, we don't know who is in on the kidnappings. The best thing we can do is act as if everybody we see is the enemy. And that includes the taxi driver. Who, by the way, bears a striking resemblance to Rosita—hatchet face, dark hovering eyebrows, facial expression that says *I'd as soon rip you apart as look at you.*

After Uncle Charlie pays the cab fare and we're left alone in front of Cozumel Palace, I reference the driver's family resemblance to Tulum's surly cook.

"I noticed," he says. "Small island, small native population. I'll look into it." Uncle Charlie hails a bellhop. "Let's get settled in, then meet in Callie's room. Say, twenty minutes." He looks Mama straight in the eye. "Ruby Nell, till then, stay out of trouble."

"I never have let you tell me what to do, Charlie Valentine. Do you think I'm going to start taking your advice at this late date?"

"Probably not. Still, it's worth a try."

I'm so glad to see the easy camaraderie has returned between Mama and my daddy's brother. There were times back during the Elvis Ultimate Tribute Artist Competition in Tupelo and during the Memphis Mambo Murders when I feared they'd alienated each other so much that we'd have an empty seat at Mama's Thanksgiving and Christmas dinners down on the farm.

Checking back into the hotel is no problem. We never checked out of our rooms. While Uncle Charlie pulls a few strings to get Mama and Fayrene switched to the room next to mine so we can keep an eye on each other—his words, not mine—I take the elevator up and walk straight back into civilization. Flat screen TV, carpet, ornate bedspread and draperies, watercolors on the walls, Jacuzzi calling my name.

It will have to wait. Twenty minutes is not time enough to do a hot tub justice.

Though everything looks the same as when I left, I enter my room cautiously, peering under the bed, inside the closets, and under the draperies for snakes and kidnappers and no-telling-what-all. Listen, I know I'm not in the middle of a B-grade movie, but I can't forget how I almost donated body parts to the Frankenstein aspirations of Morgan a.k.a. Bela Lugosi.

The coast looks clear. Usually the first thing I do is unpack my bag and hang my clothes. Not today. The first thing I do is strip off my shorts, strap on my leg holster, and change into a denim miniskirt. I view myself from all angles in the full-length mirror on the bathroom door. Satisfied the holster doesn't show, I slide a clip into the gun, heft it for balance (which makes me feel as if I know what I'm doing), and secure it in the holster.

Now I'm a hairdresser packing heat. And I'm not talking blow-dryer.

Standing in front of the mirror, I practice my draws. Clint Eastwood in Jimmy Choo stilettos. John Wayne in Bare Minerals Clear Radiance and Blush Secret.

I draw again and hit Morgan three times, twice in the groin, and once in the heart, for good measure. He's going down and I'm giving a rebel yell, when there's a knock on the door.

My watch tells me it's too early for Uncle Charlie and the gang.

"Maid service."

With my hand on the gun-size lump on my hip, I leave my phantom corpse on the carpet and move toward the door, expecting to find the ubiquitous Juanita standing there with an armload of sheets.

To my relief, the maid is an Asian teenager in pigtails, with buckteeth.

Well, I'm sure she's not really a teenager, but when your eggs are fainting from despair and you've just aged sixteen years at the hands of a kidnapper threatening to turn you into Peg Leg Pete, anybody under the age of thirty looks like a teenager.

"You called for fresh linens?" The maid holds out an armload of fluffy towels.

I'm getting ready to tell her I didn't call for linens when my instincts start screaming bloody murder. Stepping quickly into the hallway and around the startled maid, I spot a dark-haired woman vanishing into the snack room down the hall.

"Rosita!" I'd know that tacky hair anywhere. I take off running. Tulum's cook can only be in the Cozumel Palace for one reason: she's Morgan's female partner, and she's here to finish the job he started.

"Stop!" I yell, then nearly crash into a cart

emerging from the room three doors down. The tiny Mayan maid pushing it jumps back into the room and slams the door, the devil take her cart.

Pumping into high gear, I sprint toward the snack room, round the corner, and skid to a stop. Sitting at the small formica-topped table with a diet Pepsi and a pack of Nabs, Rosita looks at me as if I'm three years old and not very bright.

"Señorita?" Her unplucked eyebrows rise toward an ugly hairdo that would take a miracle for even someone of my styling talents to fix. "Is there something you wanted?"

"What are you doing here?" I know. *I know.* Not very subtle. But if you'd spent the last day chained to a bed with threats of knives and dismemberment in your immediate future, you'd ditch subtlety, too.

"Visiting my mother. Carmita." She indicates the woman beside her.

Chagrined, I notice a woman in the uniform of the Cozumel Palace maids sitting at the table. She looks old enough to be Juanita and Rosita's mother. The older woman is much darker, one hundred percent Hispanic, I'd guess, while Rosita has the café au lait coloring of someone with mixed heritage.

Rosita's companion is beautiful in the way of older women who age gracefully and well—no artifice, no makeup, no nip-tuck enhancements, just a sweet spirit that shines through her tears.

If Carmita is really the mother of the hard-as-nails Rosita, no wonder the poor woman is crying.

The least I can do is be nice to her. I introduce myself and extend my hand.

"It's lovely to meet you."

She grabs me and hangs on as if I'm a long lost friend. Then she proceeds to nod and pat my hand.

I guess that means she speaks no English. Or that she's discovered that pretending not to know what some of the guests in this hotel are saying saves her all kinds of grief. Smart woman, Rosita's mama.

Now what? I fumble in my pocket, come up with change, and get a 7-Up from the soda machine.

"Thirsty," I say. I lift the can and take a long swig. Let them think I was running because I was practically dying of thirst. Let them think I'm an ugly American who likes to make a scene wherever I go. I don't care. They don't fool me and I probably don't fool them.

"Enjoy your visit," I say, all smiles, then stroll back down the hall determined to find out more about the mysterious Carmita and why on earth the surly cook, Rosita, followed us to Cozumel.

I'm about halfway down the hall when Mama and Fayrene streak out of the adjoining room, howling. As much as I'd like to think they're hungry and racing to be first in the lunch buffet line downstairs, the one coherent word I pick up tells another story.

"Cannibals!" This from Fayrene, who streaks past me. The door to the fire stairwell bangs open and the last I see of her is the tail of her pea green housecoat disappearing into the bowels of the stairwell.

I grab Mama before she lopes past. But not before I peer down the hall toward the snack room to see how Rosita and her mother are reacting to this disturbance. They're staying out of sight.

Is that a sign of innocence or of guilt? My money is on guilt. Listen, if I'd been messing around in the room of somebody with Mama's known volatility, I'd be fully prepared for the ensuing hullabaloo. I'd sit tight with my diet Pepsi too and play blind and deaf.

"Mama, what's going on?"

"This." Mama hands me a voodoo doll riddled with pins in painful places.

Furthermore, the doll looks suspiciously like Mama, with raven hair and brightly colored caftan, Mama's usual and most distinctive garb of choice. As if that wasn't bad enough, there's a note attached that reads, *You're next.*

"You shouldn't have touched it, Mama."

"I'd like to know why not? If you think I'm going to keep this ugly thing sitting around staring at me, you're wrong."

"Uncle Charlie might be able to have prints lifted."

"Well, listen to you. I do believe my daughter's turning into a detective."

"I'd as soon turn into a fashion disaster as spend the rest of my life chasing petty criminals and major monsters."

"What you ought to do is chase Jack." Leave it to Mama to find a way to bring my love life into the conversation. I believe she could do it from the front pew of Wildwood Baptist Church in the middle of a hellfire and damnation sermon.

"That subject's off-limits."

"Flitter, nothing's off-limits with me. It comes with the territory."

"What territory?"

"Motherhood, which you'd find out if you'd let that hunk of a husband back in your house."

"Ex."

"Not yet."

I give up. But I'm not about to let on to Mama. It won't do to let her see how easy it is to win every argument with me. Lovie says I'm a pushover, that I let people take advantage of me. I'm trying to turn over a new leaf. Really, I am. The only problem is, there are so many leaves to choose from, I can't make up my mind which one to turn over first.

I lead Mama back into her room. "Listen,

we've got to find out everything we can about a maid named Carmita."

I quickly fill her in on the family reunion in the snack room.

"You're going to tell Charlie?"

"Of course. But that doesn't mean we're going to sit back and do nothing."

Mama gives me a wink and a high-five, then I pull out my cell phone to call Uncle Charlie. Within five minutes he's in the room.

"Show me exactly where you found the voodoo doll, Ruby Nell."

"Over there. Sitting on my bedside table putting the evil eye on me."

"There's no such thing as the evil eye, Mama."

"That's what you said about my inner animal, and look how that turned out."

I have to agree, but I don't tell Mama. Any further ammunition and she's going to turn completely native on me.

"Any word from Jack?" I ask my uncle.

"No, but that's a good thing."

Meaning Jack can handle anything. Meaning Jack won't call unless he's surrounded by Morgan's minions who plan to use him for target practice. Or he's fending off cannibals with a hankering for a very tough bad boy.

I wish I could control my own hankering. Sounds like leaf number one to me. As in *turning over a new . . .*

"Cal," Uncle Charlie tells me, "I found out Lulu Farkle's in charge of the seminar on 'Makeup for the Final Journey.' You need to go."

"Holy cow, is that what they're calling it?"

"Lulu's from Arkansas," Mama says, which explains everything.

We Southerners love our euphemisms. The dead never die. They *pass on, go to Glory Land, embark on a final journey, expire, head to the great tent revival in the sky.* Or as Mama is fond of engraving on tombstones at Everlasting Monuments in Mooreville, they *boogie on up to dance with the saints.* What can you expect? She's fond of the TV show, *Dancing with the Stars.*

"While you're in the makeup seminar, I'd better find Fayrene," Mama says. "She's probably halfway to Mooreville by now."

She grabs her purse and hustles out the door while I explain to Uncle Charlie about seeing Rosita and her so-called mama. Our plan is for him to follow that lead, plus others I'm sure I don't even know about, and see if he can get fingerprints from the voodoo doll, while I waltz on down to the seminar.

First I zip into my room, refresh my makeup—listen, I'm not about to attend a seminar on beauty, even if it's for the dearly departed, without looking my best—then face the mirror and do my best imitation of Rita Hayworth to Glenn Ford in the film noir classic, *Gilda.*

"If I'd been a ranch, they would've named me The Bar Nothing."

With a lethal weapon up my skirt and a recently adopted bad attitude, I head out the door to the elevator. The electronic ping announces its arrival, and I slip inside, grateful I'm alone for a few minutes. Leaning my head against the wall, I deep breathe as I glide downward.

When the doors slide open on the mezzanine, I take a slow breath and step into the midst of Cozumel's biggest party of the year, otherwise known as the undertakers' convention.

"All right, muffin, let's have a little dose of straight talk," I say to myself. (Thelma Ritter to Jean Peters in *Pickup on South Street.*)

A few people give me funny looks, but what do I care? Lulu Farkle had better watch out. Her worst nightmare is headed her way.

Chapter 20

Botched Plans, Marilyn Monroe, and a Farkle Future

Weaving through the crowd of undertakers, stylists for the deceased, and marble monument salespeople, I try to blend in. No easy feat. A woman my height—five feet, nine inches—always stands out. Not to mention that my sleek, swingy brown bob always attracts admiring glances.

Some might call it vanity, but I call it good advertising.

Over the heads of a group of portly, pasty-faced men wearing tags that identify them as hailing from Seattle, Washington, I spot Lulu Farkle, heading into Salon B. She pauses in the doorway to glance over her shoulder.

Quickly, I whirl around to hug the person behind me. A surprised Seattle citizen who calls me Julia.

"Julia! Long time, no see," he says, his big grin showing gold-capped molars.

"Indeed, how long has it been?" I try to pull myself out of his embrace, but he holds on tight.

"Too long. Let's catch up over a drink tonight. Say, six? The Turquesa?"

"Super. See you then." He releases me and I give him a little beauty queen wave. Something all my Southern female clients have down to a fine art. "Toodle-oo."

Ever since Lovie and I ended up in Las Vegas chasing the missing corpse from Uncle Charlie's funeral home, I've turned into a woman of bad habits. I can lie, break and enter, and impersonate anybody who suits my purposes at the drop of a hat. Or a corpse.

Telling myself it's all for a good cause—

finding Lovie and Elvis—and that when I get back home I'm going to ditch every one of my recently acquired bad habits and go back to being nothing but a hairstylist, I slip into the back of Salon B.

Perfect timing. The room is teeming with people, mostly female, who have come to learn the latest techniques for putting an appealing face on folks waiting for their last, long journey.

Listen, I don't think about that too much. All I know is that my skills—both with the living and the dead—make people happy, either the client or the surviving relatives.

Quickly I locate an empty chair in the back row, slide into it, and then slouch down in the hopes that Lulu won't notice me.

Fortunately, she doesn't. She's up front tapping the microphone in a way that reminds me of Mayor Robert Earl Getty back home. I almost stand up and say, *hon, it's working.*

Since I'm here without even a half-baked plan, I hunker down to see what will happen next. Lulu drones on awhile about a new line of pancake makeup. I'm about to chalk the seminar up to a lost cause when a bellhop rolls a sheet-draped gurney onto the dais. He brings it to a stop beside a table filled with familiar pots of pancake and blush.

Lulu climbs aboard, then announces that she's going to be the guinea pig while volunteers from her *esteemed audience of makeup artists*—her words, not mine—come on up and demonstrate what they're doing in their own hometowns.

"Surprise me," she yells. "I'm just going to lie down, shut my eyes, and wait for a brave volunteer."

I seize my chance. The minute Lulu lies down, a woman in the third row springs up and starts for the steps, but she doesn't stand a chance against Hair.Net's long-legged beauty goddess with a mission.

I grab a pot of pancake and tower over the unsuspecting Lulu.

"Can I peek now?" she says. I never would have put *coy* in the same sentence with Lulu Farkle.

"You can look."

Her eyes snap open and she almost comes off the gurney. I put my hand on her chest and push her back down.

Listen, in spite of Lovie's opinion that I'm all skin and bones, I work out regularly at the Wellness Center back home. I'm much stronger than I look.

"Now, now, have a little faith in your volunteer." I get a ripple of chuckles from the audience and a huge scowl from Lulu.

"What do you want?" she hisses.

"This is one feisty dearly departed," I tell the audience. To Lulu, I hiss, "Where's Lovie?"

"In hell, I hope." Lulu's latest, through clenched teeth.

I plop a big glob of pancake onto her face and cover her mouth. "We start with the base." I smile at the audience while Lulu bucks. "My corpse won't be still. Do you think I should drive a stake through her heart?"

The audience roars. Maybe there's more to being onstage than I ever knew. Maybe the heady, triumphant feeling is why Lovie always lobbied for the lead in school plays.

"Blend well." I keep Lulu relatively immobile while I use both hands to smear pancake. "Oops. Missed a spot." Leaning close, I whisper. "Why do you hate her?"

"She spoiled the plan."

"What plan?" Still hovering close, I pretend to be taking great pains to cover every inch of Lulu's bad skin so she can go on to Glory Land looking more like *Beauty* than *the Beast*.

"The merger with Charlie. A chain of Farkle Funeral Homes."

Uncle Charlie would never consider a merger with anybody, let alone Alvin Farkle. Though he's never interfered with Lovie's love life, I know for a fact that he didn't cotton to the idea of his only daughter hooking up with a man he considered lacking not only in manners but also in skills as a funeral director.

A few women in the front row are leaning

forward in their chairs, apparently catching on that there's more taking place on the dais than a simple makeup demonstration.

I bedazzle my audience with a smile. I hope.

"Sorry about that. I was catching up on news about Lulu's brother, Alvin. What a hunk."

"Die in hell," she hisses.

"You first." I tell her, all smiles and good cheer, as I hold her mouth shut with one hand, uncap a lipstick with the other, and paint her surly lips in a perfect cupid's bow, à la Marilyn Monroe.

Listen, I'm a natural. Most people take years to learn what I sprang from the womb knowing. Give me a few pots of paint and some tubes of lipstick, and I can make the deceased look so good they practically rise up and shout.

A few whisks of mascara, a strategic sweep of blush, and Lulu Farkle looks better than she ever has.

I release her and she pops up, looking ready to claw my eyes out. The audience bursts into applause, which takes her by surprise.

While she's still sitting on the gurney, undecided about whether to run or to turn me over to hotel security, I clamp my hands on her shoulders from behind, then lean in as if I'm going to kiss her cheek.

"Did Alvin take my cousin?"

"He wouldn't take her back if she begged." The

audience is still giving us a standing ovation. "As far as we're concerned, she can take Eternal Rest and stick it where it doesn't show."

"Charming." I smile at the audience.

"Likewise, I'm sure." She takes a bow.

While she's clamboring off the gurney, taking another bow, I slip toward the back and ease out the door. Within seconds, I disappear (I hope) into the crowd trying to get to the coffee urns and cookies in the mezzanine.

Now I know why the Farkles hate Lovie. Lulu was bound to be telling the truth. Nobody could come up with such a fantastic tale on such short notice. Especially under the circumstances.

Obviously, Alvin needed Uncle Charlie's reputation—and probably money—to launch his plan. As one of the senior undertakers and a past president of funeral directors on both the state and national levels, Uncle Charlie commands the respect of his colleagues all over the U.S.

I can just imagine why Lovie never told me about the proposed chain of Farkle Funeral Homes. She wouldn't have been able to quit laughing long enough.

I'm fixing to call Uncle Charlie to report my findings, when my cell phone rings. It's Fayrene.

"Callie, come quick."

"What's up?"

"Ruby Nell's been hijacked."

Holy cow! I try to get a grip on myself.

Morgan's in jail, Uncle Charlie's on the island, and undertakers are everywhere. How could Mama vanish in the midst of all that?

Besides, Fayrene tends to overreact and exaggerate, and that's putting it mildly. "You've got to hurry, Callie. I'm about prostate with worry."

"Where are you?"

"Right here where Ruby Nell said."

"I can't find you unless you're more specific, Fayrene."

"At the bar on the beach, having a Tropical Double Trouble."

Holy cow! That's the near same spot where Lovie vanished.

Grabbing two cookies off one of the refreshment tables scattered about, I hurry through the mezzanine while trying to look nonchalant.

Listen, just because I got by with that stunt in Salon B, I'm not home free yet. Any minute now, Lulu Farkle could descend on me with a security guard.

Or worse. Her brother. Alvin Farkle. Who might have taken Lovie, and now Mama. All on account of the unfortunate Farkle Funeral Home chain.

Hysterical laughter bubbles up. I wonder if I'm falling apart.

Elvis' Opinion #14 on
Silly Lyrics, Silk Scarves, and Rescue the Perishing

Well, bless'a my soul. Now that I've got the attention of the natives with my rendition of "King of the Whole Wide World," I've got to do a follow-up.

They leave behind their traps and nets and ropes and come storming toward me like a bunch of frenzied females from one of my Las Vegas concerts, looking for one of my sweat-soaked scarves.

I take a bow and treat the natives to a curled lip. *Thank you, thank you very much.*

Though I'm an icon who can steal the stage from anybody, I've got sense enough to know a few bows won't satisfy my Mayan fans for long. I do a quick turn that makes my mismatched ears spin, then strike a flattering pose before I launch into "I'll Never Let You Go (Little Darlin')."

Before you start thinking that's a weird song choice, let me explain a thing or two. Number one, these dudes don't speak English. Number two, there's nothing to this phrase I'm singing to confuse the natives. All I'm saying is "well'a, well'a, well'a," which with my drawl—sounds like walla, walla, walla. I got a big laugh when I explained that to my audience at the June 1975 concert in Dallas, Texas.

I'm getting the same laughs now. Plus, applause and the usual imitators. Natives start spinning and swirling every which way, some of them picking up the chant, "Well'a, well'a, well'a."

What can I say? The King lives! Satisfied that I've put to rest any lingering suspicions about my motives—like, *I'm casing this joint so I can get out of here*—I take another bow, then sashay my transcendent self back toward the hut.

But let me tell you, the scent I pick up stops me cold. Lifting my famous nose, I take another whiff. I'd know that scent anywhere.

Jack. Not too far away and getting closer by the minute.

He's most likely armed and he's definitely dangerous. Trust me. If I know my human daddy—and I most certainly do—he'll strike with the same stealth and cunning of his code name—Black Panther.

Shagging my ample self into gear, I race into the hut to tell Lovie. The sight I behold halts me in my tracks. This place looks like it's been bombed with flowers. Big, exotic blooms are everywhere—covering the throne, festooning the support poles, banked around the perimeter, and even piled up on my personal sleeping mat.

But where's Lovie?

I throw back my handsome basset head and howl, "Hey Little Girl."

An arm emerges. Then a leg.

"Elvis, stop that racket and help me out of this funeral bouquet."

Now she's talking. Listen, in this dog's life, digging is what I do best.

With Lovie's muscle and my four good paws, it doesn't take long before we've unearthed the goddess of the Earth and Moon.

I nearly jump out of my dog suit. With her painted-on tigress face and dark, dangerous-looking blooms dripping from every crevice and corner, Lovie's not somebody you'd want to meet in the dark.

"If I ever get out of here, I'm going to kill somebody. Just about anybody will do."

I lick her feet to show I couldn't agree more.

"Tonight, Elvis. I don't care what's out there in the jungle. It can't be as bad as staying cooped up here divining the sex of babies."

I try to think of the best way to say *we're fixing to spring this joint,* but the only song that comes to mind is "Here Comes Santa Claus."

Clutching an imaginary microphone in my paw, I howl a few bars.

"Elvis, have you lost your mind?"

I do a second verse to show her I'm serious as sin.

Lovie's not listening. Furthermore, she's not

buying it. Maybe that Mayan brew did some damage I don't know about.

I'm casting about for a way to tell her, *Jack is coming,* when outside events render my problem moot. (You didn't think I knew lawyer talk, did you? Listen, I'm a dog of many talents. You don't even want to know.)

From the direction of the jungle comes an unholy howling. Natives on the warpath.

And then, Jack's counterpoint bellow of pure outrage.

"What's that?" Lovie races out of the hut with me right behind her.

Streaming flowers and bad attitude, we hustle across the compound just in time to see six natives marching into the village bearing their latest prize: Jack Jones on a litter, his right leg shattered by a jaguar trap.

They set him in the middle of the compound, then race off to tell Somebody in Charge. Probably the old lady who speaks English.

All I can think of is a medley of "Hard Luck," "Hard Knocks," and "Help Me."

Looks like if anybody's going to "Rescue the Perishing," it's all up to me.

Chapter 21

High Stakes, Hijinks, and Hardened Criminals

No sooner have I set foot on the beach in front of the hotel than Fayrene spots me and streaks my way.

"Yoohoo! Callie!" Lest I fail to see her, she waves her arms and keeps calling as she comes.

In cabbage green pedal pushers with matching blouse and a green Panama hat the size of a bale of hay, she's impossible to miss. As a matter of fact, half the people on the beach turn to wave at her and call out *Yoohoo!*

This is nothing new to me. When you're kin to Mama and friends with Fayrene, daily public displays come with the package.

A breeze has sprung up. If the wind gets under her hat, Fayrene's liable to sail all the way to Arkansas. I catch her arm as she whizzes by and then lead her to a couple of beach chairs protected from the breeze and nosey beachcombers by a tamale stand.

"When did you last see Mama?"

She consults her watch. "Exactly one hour and fifteen minutes ago."

"That's hardly enough time to say someone

took her. Did you see any suspicious-looking characters around? Alvin or Lulu Farkle? Rosita?"

"No, but I know. It's my ESPN."

Holy cow! If my last nerve snaps, I won't be responsible for what I do. At least, though, I can relax about Mama a bit.

"That's hardly a basis to claim kidnapping."

"She said she'd meet me here fifteen minutes ago. Ruby Nell is always punctuated."

Oh, great. Fifteen minutes is even less time to cry *foul play.*

"What was Mama doing? How'd you two get separated?"

"After she caught up with me, I was changing clothes when that maid came in, that Carmita you said for us to find out about. Well, she and Ruby Nell got to talking . . ."

"Wait a minute. I don't think Carmita speaks English and I know Mama doesn't speak Spanish."

"I don't know where you got that idea. Ruby Nell's been practicing Spanish ever since Charlie invited her to the undertakers' convention, and that Carmita was talking English up a storm."

"So, what happened?"

"The first thing I know, Ruby Nell said she was heading to *the back room* with Carmita and she'd meet me at the beach bar in an hour." Fayrene taps her watch as a witness. "On the dot."

"The back room? Do you have any idea where that is?"

"I don't know, and I didn't ask. Bobby Huckabee told me I was in danger from a dark-eyed señorita, so I stayed behind to man the port."

The only good thing I can say about all this is that Bobby has upgraded his prediction. After telling Fayrene to call Uncle Charlie with the latest development, then wait for me in her room, I head back to the hotel to discover the whereabouts of "the back room."

Thanks to corpses that won't stay put and dead Elvis impersonators and dancers who dive off rooftops, I'm no stranger to sleuthing. If you want to locate a slightly shady back room, you ask a slightly shady character.

Though a few of the undertakers fit the bill, I don't think HI, I'M BILL FROM CALIFORNIA can help me. Ditto HI, I'M LEON FROM TEXAS.

I'm skulking around the lobby, trying to locate sleazy characters when I notice the cab driver who picked us up at the ferry, parked outside the entrance. Lurking is a better word. There's something about the way he's slouched behind the wheel studying the tourists that makes me want to offer him a toothbrush and soap and enroll him in a Dale Carnegie course.

Trying to appear casual, I saunter his way. If I had one of Mama's cigarettes, I could create the perfect character—a whole lot bored, a little bit wild, and looking for trouble.

"Hi," I lean in the window. "I'm looking for a little action around here."

"Move on, lady. All I do is drive a cab."

Something about his eyes tells another story.

I peel a ten out of my pocket and pass it to him. "I've heard the back room is where I want to be."

"How bad do you want to be there?"

I hand him another ten and he spits out the window. I come up with another ten, my last.

He wads the bills into his pocket, and nods toward the hotel. "Basement. Down the stairs, past the laundry, and turn right. Can't miss it."

I'd ask him what's going on in the back room, but that would be pushing my luck. Ostensibly, I already know. And, in any case, I'll soon find out.

I start to walk off, then remember who I'm supposed to be and add a swing to my sashay. Lovie would approve. She believes in flaunting your natural assets.

Losing myself in the lobby crowd, I angle toward the stairs and push open the door. The stairwell is poorly lit and creepy. I pat my holster just to reassure myself that I've still got a deadly weapon up my skirt.

I try for stealth, but in the concrete and metal enclosure, the echo of my footsteps could wake the dead.

Suddenly I freeze. It sounds like I am not alone.

Listen, the way these last few days have turned out, I wouldn't be surprised to stumble over a corpse on the stairs or have something half-dead waiting around the corner.

I ease out my gun and hold it in front of me with both hands, just like Jack taught me in my other life as wife to the sexiest man on the planet.

I'm not even going to go there.

Unfortunately, my posturing won't make up for the fact that I can't hit the side of a barn, let alone a tin can off Mama's pasture fence. Creeping down the final few stairs, I step into a narrow hallway and ease toward the sound.

Did the cab driver say right or left? I'm so nervous I can't remember. Using my cousin's favorite decision-making process, I whisper, *Eenie, meenie, minie, moe.*

I turn right and discover the monster lurking around the corner—an industrial-size dryer whose load has shifted and is knocking the machine around.

Light spills from a half-open doorway down the hall. Heading that way, I hear another sound—Mama's laughter. A good sign. I ease my gun down to my side and step into the room.

There's Mama, cards in one hand, cigarette holder in the other, and half my after-Thanksgiving shoe budget on the table.

She looks up. "It's just my daughter. Bet or pass."

I'm as close as I've ever been to saying one of Lovie's words when I notice that one of the back room gamblers is Carmita.

"Callie, let me introduce you to my friends. This handsome fellow is Raoul from the kitchen, next to him is Pete from Texas, and I believe you know Carmita."

I hide my gun behind my back and tell everybody hello. Then, "Mama, we need to talk."

"Just a minute." She spreads her cards on the table, says, "Full house," then rakes in my money.

Thank goodness. At the rate she's going, I ought to let her play another hand or two. Maybe I'll get my loan back. A first.

She grabs her loot, says, "Toodle-ooo. See ya'll later," and we get out of there before somebody sees that I've got a gun and Mama was there to snoop.

There's no telling what back room regulars do if they discover you've entered their game under false pretenses. At least, I hope Mama's were false.

As soon as we've gained the stairs, I ask her.

"You did go down there to find out about Carmita?"

"Ha."

"Mama, that's not a word. And since when have you ever said *ya'll*."

261

"It's part of my Southern belle disguise. I didn't want them to catch on that I'm a seasoned private eye who could take them all down."

I don't point out that Mama's not a private eye and that the only thing she takes down with any regularity is my bank account. We have to move fast. Any minute now we could be chased by back room losers or Lulu Farkle still mad about her Marilyn Monroe makeup and her failed chain of Farkle Funeral Homes.

We race to the top of the stairs, and I'm proud to say that Mama doesn't miss a beat. Listen, I've got some good genes. Between my daily exercise regimes and Mama's DNA, I could become an entry in the *Guinness Book of World Records*—the woman whose eggs got fertilized after everybody in Mooreville had dropped her from the prayer list.

We push through to the lobby and collapse into a couple of wing chairs overlooking the beach.

"What did you find out, Mama?"

"You'll never guess Juanita and Rosita's father."

"Holy cow, Mama. I don't want to play guessing games."

"Archie Morgan."

"That explains why Juanita would deck herself out in sheets and help her daddy chase off Rocky's crew."

"Not Juanita. Rosita. She forced her sister into helping her with the sheets."

"Was Rosita the one who helped kidnap me?"

"We didn't get that far. Raoul and Pete came in and I couldn't very well talk about kidnapping in front of them."

"If Rosita's involved, she's probably keeping it from her mother."

"Flitter, Carolina. You can't keep anything from a mother."

That would strike terror to my heart if I didn't already know that what Mama says is true. Listen, when Jack left, she knew before I even called her, even before Mooreville's grapevine got a whiff. Don't ask me how.

I'm in the middle of telling Mama that Fayrene's waiting in their room when Uncle Charlie rings my cell phone.

"Jack's found Lovie and Elvis." I burst into tears. Extreme happiness always does that to me. "Meet me on the beach. The Company's sending a helicopter."

"I can go, too?"

"Jack needs you. Hurry. I'll explain later."

I might pass out from anxiety. I give Mama only the good news, but I also give her a job to do. Mama hates being left out.

"Call Darlene and Bobby. Let them know Jack found Lovie and Elvis."

"Darlene and Bobby, my hind foot. We're calling everybody in Mooreville."

The first thing I see when I step outside is the chopper that dominates the beach, its blades beating the air. Uncle Charlie spots me, ducks down, and races to my side.

"Come, dear heart. We don't have a minute to lose."

"Jack?"

"We're airlifting him to the hospital."

"Alive?"

"Yes. He sounded strong on the phone."

I hurry into the chopper, then collapse against Uncle Charlie as it lifts off, destination unknown. At least to me.

We're out over the Caribbean before I notice that I'm traveling with twin Incredible Hulks—men so large they look as if they could bench press Texas before breakfast and then jog to Canada and back before supper. Two men I wouldn't want to meet in the dark—or anywhere else—without Uncle Charlie or Jack Jones.

Well, there you have it. Jack Jones, who at this very moment may be lying somewhere in the jungle bleeding and torn limb from limb and no-telling-what-all, is always on my mind.

Listen, with that kind of mindset, I'm in the wrong business. I ought to give up beauty and become a country-and-western singer.

"Uncle Charlie?" I nod my head in the direction of the twin Abominable Snowmen.

"Company men."

No use to ask more. He won't tell, and quite frankly, I don't want to know.

All I can say is that since I'm going into hostile territory with nothing but the weapon under my skirt, I'm glad these two are my backup.

Elvis' Opinion #15 on Diplomacy, Jaguar Traps, and Explorer Dog

While I'm licking my human daddy's face, Lovie races toward us in full goddess regalia.

"Jack. Thank god you came." She glances around, obviously searching for the man she expected to storm out of the jungle, barrels blazing, to rescue her. "Where's Rocky?"

"On a wild goose chase with Seth."

Lovie says a word that would cauterize wounds. "When I get my hands on them, they're both dead."

"Who kidnapped you, Lovie?"

Two natives grab her before she can finger the criminal. I try to tell him with a hasty version of "Devil in Disguise," but all bedlam has broken loose.

The natives are screeching, and Lovie's spitting and clawing. If you think the makeup brought out the tigress in Lovie, think again. She's been a jungle cat since she turned fourteen (the year her mama died and a heartbroken Charlie left his daughter to her own resources).

Just because these villagers are not a bunch of warriors who practice ancient murderous rituals, that doesn't mean they plan to sit back and twiddle their thumbs while they lose their long lipped god as well as their Earth and Moon goddess.

If Jack had left things to me, Explorer Dog would have had Lovie out of here tonight. As it stands, all his well-honed skills were no match for a jaguar trap.

He's trying to get up and quell the natives, but he's lost too much blood. Besides, he's all tied up.

I try to warn Lovie to cool it, by howling a few bars of "Stay Away, Joe," but she's in full Lovie mode. Nothing can stop her now. Except yours truly.

Flattening my ears and sucking in my portly stomach, I light into the wad of humanity. I know I could bare my teeth, nip a few heels, take a chunk of flesh here and there, but I'm basically peaceable by nature. I'm a diplomatic dog. I much prefer building a "Bridge Over Troubled Water" to fisticuffs.

Finally I restore some order. Listen, these

natives might not pay homage to the King, but they're very fond of their long lipped god.

"It's high time somebody came to my rescue. Even if it's not the man I was going to let discover my Holy Grail." Lovie straightens her feathers and marches over to grab my human daddy's hand. "Take me out of here, Jack. I've got scores to settle."

"I'm a bit tied up right now."

The natives have bound him, hand and foot. Plus, they've followed Lovie, and now they're surrounding us.

Never show your fear. I shake my ample hips at them, curl my lip and howl, *well'a, well'a, well'a.*

All of a sudden the natives take up the chant.

" 'Little Darlin' in the Yucatan jungle?" Jack says. His color is fading fast, but thankfully, not his sense of humor.

"Blame Elvis," Lovie tells him.

"What's going on, Lovie?"

She briefs Jack about our status as gods and speculates that the natives are getting ready to turn him into their next living idol.

As the dog who has seen it all, I can vouch for that. Especially if these natives get a gander at Jack all cleaned up. He's a fine figure of a man. Reminds me of myself when I was wearing black leather in my comeback concert and had women fainting at my feet.

Considering my skills as a dog of diplomacy, not to mention talent, I'm not worried about Jack's becoming a god. I can do some fancy howling and set these natives straight on that score. If anybody is all man, it's Jack Jones. It won't take me long to convince the locals he's not woo-woo god material.

My most pressing concern, though, is the state of Jack's injury. If that leg doesn't get some attention fast, my human dad is liable to end up losing a limb.

And let me tell you, I don't want to be on or near the premises when somebody tells him.

I prance my ample self over to the only native in the village who speaks English—the little old woman who was in the hut with the pregnant girls demanding Lovie's skill as a diviner of unborn-baby gender. I'm going to grab ahold of her bony ankles and not let go till she gets the idea that it's time to quit trying to turn Americans into gods and let's us get back to our pickled pigs' lips, back yard barbecues, and Rock 'n' Roll.

I'm fixing to haul off and chomp her leg when suddenly my mismatched ears pick up the sound of my master. Speaking fluent Mayan.

Leaning on one elbow, his hair plastered to his forehead with sweat, Jack has the natives mesmerized. I hope he's explaining that Lovie's and my god days are over. I think he's explaining that we're leaving now, and there's not a doggoned thing the villagers can do about it.

It's my fondest hope that he's also asking the cook to go straight to the kitchen and fetch me a little smackeral of something good for the trip.

I have to say, I'm proud of my human daddy. He's got the whole village in the palm of his hand.

All of a sudden, I hear the sweetest sound this side of Mooreville.

Chopper blades. Thanks to Jack's quick thinking, I'm sure. He'd have called for backup the minute he sensed trouble.

Lifting my handsome head, I put my eyes to the sky and see my human mom in the helicopter, waving down at me, her face streaked with tears and split with a smile that's the stuff of Jack Jones' dreams.

Chapter 22

Wild Goose Chase,
Return to Civilization,
and Captives on the Warpath

From the helicopter, the scene below looks like something from a blockbuster Indiana Jones movie—tiny Mayan Indians in colorful native garb, Lovie in feathers and war paint, Jack trussed like somebody they plan to burn at the stake, and Elvis with his floppy ears flying outward. I don't know who I'm the happiest to see. Well, all of them, really.

But when the chopper sets down, Elvis is the first one in my arms. He leaps up and starts licking my face, and I vow on the spot never to lose him again.

Over the top of his head I wave at Lovie. Screaming her name, I head her way, but suddenly I'm hemmed in and grabbed by little people who are either happy to see me or plan to eat me for dinner.

I glance around for Uncle Charlie, but he and the Hulks are hustling Jack into the chopper. Thank goodness.

Suddenly Lovie gives a rebel yell and lights into the natives, snatching and shoving my captors until my cousin and I are the only ones standing. With her feathers and flowers askew and her fierce war paint melting in the sun, she's never looked more beautiful to me.

"Back off," she snarls, "or I'm going to turn you into a village of toads."

I grab my cousin and think I won't be able to let go until Christmas.

"Lovie, did anybody hurt you? Are you okay? What happened? I was worried sick about you."

"Are you kidding me? If anybody had tried to lay a hand on me, there'd be a pile of dead bodies all the way from here to Cozumel."

I'm relieved to see that the cousin I know and love is completely intact. But what did I expect? This is Lovie we're talking about.

Grabbing her by the hand, I say, "Come on, Lovie. Let's get out of here."

Out of the corner of my eye, I see Elvis has already trotted after Jack and is waiting by the helicopter. Like Mama, he thinks my ex walks on water. One of the Hulks reaches down to lift Elvis aboard.

"Wait a minute." Lovie strikes a pose. "I've got something to do first."

Holy cow! What now?

Swooping in a circle that sends flowers and feathers flying, she looks like a molting wild bird. While the natives are on their hands and knees picking up the scattered blossoms, Lovie lifts her arms over her head.

"Blessings from the goddess of Earth and Moon," she shouts. "Long may your little pea-picking hearts prosper."

The villagers start shouting something back that I believe is an ancient Mayan chant. Lacing my arms through my cousin's, I lead her toward the helicopter.

Behind us the chant begins to sound suspiciously like "well'a, well'a, well'a."

"Little Darlin'" in the middle of the Mayan jungle? That can't be right. I know extreme stress can contribute to all kinds of bizarre illnesses. I wonder if it can cause you to hear things.

Lovie clambers aboard and I'm right behind her. I'm sorry to report that it's impossible to be graceful climbing into a helicopter in a short skirt while trying to maintain decorum and hide a gun.

When I finally get aboard, the first thing I see is Jack, looking as pale as old man Morgan in his sheet. He winks at me. Knowing he was watching for—and probably saw—a glimpse of glory, as Lovie would say, I kneel beside him and take his hand.

Listen, I may be trying to make *no* my middle name where Jack's concerned, but I'm still the same compassionate woman who encourages my clients at Hair.Net to come to me with all their problems and sordid secrets.

"Jack, don't you dare die on me."

"I wouldn't dream of it, Cal." Just when I'm thinking he's going to get the wrong idea, and I'm wondering whether I should release him and sit with Uncle Charlie, my almost-ex says, "I've got divorce papers to sign."

"You bet your britches," I tell him. But I keep on holding his hand.

Blood is my excuse. His. Which is rapidly soaking through his pants and dripping onto my shoes.

I glance toward the front of the chopper, where

Lovie and Uncle Charlie are deep in conversation.

"Hurry," I tell my uncle, but by the time the words are out of my mouth, the chopper is hovering over the island and setting down on the hospital rooftop. Jack is whisked off by men in white.

While I'm standing on the rooftop wondering if I ought to call Mama first or find the waiting room, we're approached by a severe-looking woman with her hair pulled back so tight her eyes are little slits.

"Mr. Valentine?" Her nametag identifies her as Sonia Mendoza, the hospital administrator, no less. "Right this way. We have a room for you."

The formidable Sonia gives Elvis a look that means she's not too happy that he's part of the Valentine party, but I tell her, "He goes, too," and that's that.

She escorts us to a board room, from the looks of it—long, polished table, plush leather chairs, coffee and doughnuts on a mahogany credenza.

I'm famished. While Sonia and Uncle Charlie stand in the doorway in quiet conversation, Lovie and I fall on the doughnuts. I put two on a plate for Elvis. Forget his diet. He's earned some fat and sugar.

After Sonia leaves, Uncle Charlie joins us.

"Rocky and Seth Alford will be here shortly. Lovie, they don't know you've been found. I don't want them to see you until they're in this room and the door is closed."

"What in the world's going on?" I ask. "Rocky's not part of Morgan's ugly scheme."

"No, but Seth Alford is, the sorry snake. When he took me off the beach I was so sloshed I could have mistaken him for Santa Claus. By the time I came back to my senses, I knew it was Seth. When I get my hands on him, he's going to be nothing but a greasy spot."

For once, Uncle Charlie doesn't pat Lovie and say *now, now, dear heart.* If I had my guess, I'd say he'll have to use every bit of his restraint to keep from doing bodily harm to the man who did this to Lovie.

"Rosita's fingerprints were all over the voodoo doll. She's already been picked up," Uncle Charlie says. "Jack and I have suspected Seth for some time."

"Why?" I ask. "He seemed so nice."

"He's Morgan's nephew, and the two of them have been after the lost tomb for years. They knew Rocky was close. In order to get credit, they had to get him out of the way. They thought kidnapping Lovie would do the job."

"It should have. Rocky Malone should have been combing the jungle day and night. Forget the lost tomb. He ought to have been tending his lost love."

"He was desperate after you were kidnapped,

Lovie," I tell her. "I've never seen a man so distraught."

Rocky's really a sweet guy. Somebody has to defend him.

Lovie is not mollified. "I don't know whether I want to give him a piece of my mind first or strangle him."

I would tell her it's just a lover's quarrel that will blow over, but Lovie's still wearing war paint. Under the circumstances, I think it best if I keep my mouth shut.

"Has anybody told Mama?"

"I called her," Uncle Charlie says. "I told her to wait with Fayrene at the hotel until we get there."

"She won't listen. She never does."

"Yes, she will," Uncle Charlie says.

I'm so glad to see the twinkle back in his eye that I don't take the time to wonder why he's so certain Mama will do what he tells her. The older I get, the less I understand my mama. And my uncle, it turns out.

Footsteps echo in the hall and all of us freeze.

"Quick." Uncle Charlie nods toward a chair behind the door, and Lovie scoots in.

I prefer to stand. I want to see Seth Alford's face when he realizes his goose is cooked. Besides, I've got a gun. I don't care if this is a hospital and I am the most horrible shot in the South. If he makes a run for it, I'm going to shoot him.

Rocky is the first through the door. He looks horrible, poor man. "You said Jack's been hurt."

"That's unfortunate." Seth strolls in and smiles at me. "He should have searched where I told him instead of chasing off on his own. The jungle's a dangerous place."

"Not nearly as dangerous as this room, you lying shit." Lovie steps from behind the door and Seth turns chalky.

Like a man shell-shocked, Rocky glances from Seth to Lovie. Then he strides toward my cousin.

"Stop right there, Rocky Malone. Do you think I want a man who values the lost tomb more than he does his lost national treasure?"

"If I were you," Seth says, "I'd listen to her, Rocky. She's crazy as a loon. People lost in the jungle almost never come back with their full senses."

I never thought Seth would try to bluff his way out of this. Why doesn't Uncle Charlie say something? Is he waiting for Seth to incriminate himself?

And why hasn't Rocky jumped on him and beat the snot out of him? No wonder Lovie's miffed.

"By the way, Lovie. We're glad you're back." Seth has the audacity to blow a kiss at her.

The room goes quiet. If fury were a country, Lovie would be China. Any minute now, she's going to jump on her kidnapper and I don't think even Uncle Charlie can stop her.

Suddenly there's a low growl. *Elvis.* Something's wrong.

When Seth darts to the door, I'm the first to react. Maybe it was my dog's warning growl. Maybe it's because I'm facing the culprit who snatched Lovie and my dog.

In a move worthy of Clint Eastwood, I whip out my gun, aim with both hands, and shoot.

Seth goes down in a howl, blood blooming on his pants.

I stand there numb while Uncle Charlie takes the gun from my hands, cleans it with his handkerchief, and kneels to put it in Seth's hands.

While I'm trying to decide whether to get hysterical or thank my lucky stars for Uncle Charlie, two security guards burst into the room, guns drawn.

"The man on the floor is wanted for kidnapping," Uncle Charlie tells them. "You'll want to get him seen about his wound before he goes to jail. He was so distraught he shot himself in the groin."

Holy cow! I've ruined Seth Alford's *family.* I guess I ought to feel awful about that, but I don't. I'm just glad to have my dog and my family back.

One leaf I don't have to turn over is gratitude. I know how to be thankful I love and I am loved.

Elvis' Opinion #16 on Mooreville Homecoming, Mayan Calendar, and a Whole Lotta Hanky Panky Going On

Thanks to Jarvetis, who issued daily bulletins to the home front regarding our tropical double trouble, yours truly and crew get a hero's welcome. Darlene has banners stretched across the front of Hair.Net, Jarvetis has helium-filled balloons tied to the gas tanks, and Mooreville Feed and Seed is serving cookies and punch with every purchase of dog food and Yard Guard mosquito spray.

Even Bobby Huckabee has put up signs. Though I'll have to say his WELCOME HOME signs on the lawn of Eternal Rest Funeral Home are getting mixed reviews from the friends and relatives of the newly deceased. Charlie's so busy fielding irate phone calls, he hardly has time to put into practice the new techniques he learned in the last few days of the undertakers' convention in Cozumel.

Fayrene and Ruby Nell have taken up consulting the Mayan calendar and wearing feathers—earrings, hair ornaments, necklaces—anywhere they can put them. Last I heard, they were busy planning seminars in the back room of Gas, Grits, and Guts on "finding your inner animal."

But the biggest changes are with this intrepid jungle explorer dog and the Valentine cousins. Though Callie advises otherwise, Lovie never did patch it up with poor, befuddled Rocky. She left him in Tulum, almost too devastated to continue his search for the lost tomb. And she vows he'll never get another chance to find her national treasure.

Even if I were a gambling dog, I wouldn't place bets on this one. Lovie's as stubborn as they come, but Rocky doesn't strike me as the kind of man who will give up.

And then there's my human mom. Callie brought Jack back home, but only to take care of him until his leg heals and he can take care of himself. Or so she says.

Listen, I saw how she stayed at that hospital in Cozumel night and day till the doctors said the surgery was successful. (Jack's out of the woods and he's going to be like brand-new again.)

As you know, I'm a keen observer of human nature, especially when it happens to be the two humans I love best. Let me tell you, nothing has changed between them. Except now he's issuing daily and irritating love advice to Callie, who is determined to ignore him and pursue happiness with Champ.

I'm not too worried about the outcome. Wait till Jack's a hundred percent again. Then we'll see who Callie really wants.

Anyhow, I don't have time to fret over my human parents. I've my own love problems. Would you believe that sawed-off Lhasa escape artist has been courting Ann-Margret and trying to take over as poppa to my offspring? Even worse, my own private and personal French poodle has been making eyes right back at the "Devil in Disguise."

All this according to my own grapevine, Javetis' best redbone hound dog and my best friend, Trey.

If that useless-tailed William keeps messing with the King's sweetie, he's going to get about two inches gnawed off his three-inch legs.

Trey says no French poodle is worth fighting over, but who said anything about fighting? Listen, a dog of my talent and iconic status doesn't need to use force. Curled lips, swiveling hips, and a howling rendition of "Love Me Tender" should do the trick.

Elvis has left the building.

Lovie's Southern Fixin's

Ham and Biscuit

Country Cured Ham (I use Miller's Biscuit Strips)
Biscuits (recipe below)

While biscuits are cooking, heat a small amount of canola oil in the skillet to medium temperature. Add very thin, very lean slices of country cured ham and heat about two minutes per side (more if you like a crispier piece of ham).

Lovie's Gluten-Free Biscuits

1 cup of Bob's Red Mill Biscuit and Baking Mix
  (Gluten-Free)
2 T. unsalted butter
2 heaping T. of sour cream (do not used reduced
  fat)
9 T. 2 percent milk
Buttered or biscuit pan

Put biscuit mix in a small bowl and make a well in the center of the mix. (Don't sift.) Melt 2 T. butter in the microwave. Mix together the melted butter, sour cream, and 2 T. of milk. Pour the liquid mixture into the well you've made in the

Red Mill dry mix. Stir until the Red Mill mix has a grainy consistency. Add the rest of the milk in small increments until the batter forms a soft ball and leaves the side of the bowl. Don't over-mix. If you need more milk, add only a small amount at a time.

Sprinkle a dough board with Bob's Red Mill Gluten-Free Biscuit mix. Turn your dough ball onto the board and pat until you have a circle of dough approximately ¼ to ½ an inch high. Cut into circles with biscuit cutter. Melt a small amount of butter (not too much) in the biscuit pan, dredge both sides of the biscuits in the butter, then bake for 15 minutes in a preheated 350-degree oven. Makes about 10 biscuits.

Don't wait for the biscuits to brown. Gluten-free mix does not brown in the same manner as wheat flour. Your finished gluten-free biscuit should be just barely beginning to turn light golden.

This dough freezes well. Freeze already cut biscuits on a cookie tin until firm, then drop frozen biscuits into a plastic freezer bag. When ready to use, take out as many as you want, let thaw about fifteen minutes, the bake as usual.

Note from Elvis: The author, Peggy Webb, has to eat a gluten-free diet. After trying several mixes and following instructions on the package, she came up with biscuits hard enough to knock a bull in the head. With a lot of help from yours truly, she finally created this really good gluten-free biscuit.

Trey Webb's Nassau Grits

Instant Grits
1 lb. of bacon
1 14.5 oz. can of sliced tomatoes
1 large green bell pepper
1 large onion
½ stick of butter

In a large pot on the top of the stove, cook enough instant grits to serve eight according to directions on package, adding ½ stick of butter to the water before you cook. Turn the heat off under the cooked grits while you prepare the other ingredients.

Cook 1 lb. of bacon till crisp. Crumble bacon and set aside. Reserve bacon grease. Chop 1 bell pepper and 1 onion, and sauté both in bacon grease. Set aside.

Add 1 can of tomatoes with its juice to the grits. Add the crumbled bacon, the sautéed bell peppers and onions, and ALL the bacon grease. Mix all ingredients into the grits and serve piping hot.

Note from Elvis: Trey Webb is the author's son and one of the best doggoned cooks in the South. This is not a recipe for the fainthearted.

As Trey says, "Adding butter is optional, but it's always helpful." Delicious, too, might I add! And guess who is named after Trey in the mysteries? My best buddy, Jarvetis Johnson's redbone hound dog, Trey!

Mama's Down Home Peach Cobbler

1 stick of butter
1 14.5 oz. can of sliced peaches in sweetened juice
1 cup of self-rising flour
1 cup of sugar
1 cup of milk, whole or 2 percent (Do not use skim.)

In an 8 x 8 inch glass baking dish, melt 1 stick of butter. Set aside.

Mix together 1 cup of self-rising flour and 1 cup of sugar. Add 1 cup of milk. Stir until smooth. (For variety, you can use ¾ cup of milk and ¼ cup of juice from the peaches. This makes the cobbler a bit chewier but very, very good.)

This batter will be very thin. Slowly pour it into the melted butter in the casserole dish. DO NOT STIR.

Drain the can of peaches. Fork one slice at a time into the casserole dish on top of the batter. DO NOT STIR. Arrange slices until the top of the cobbler is covered. Use all the peaches.

Bake in a preheated 350-degree oven till the cobbler is light golden brown and a fork inserted in the center comes out clean. This will take about 30 minutes. Do not overcook. Serve hot with a topping of vanilla ice cream.

Note from Elvis: This is an old family recipe handed down from the author's mother, who lived on her farm until shortly before her death. Guess which character is modeled on Peggy's feisty mom? Ruby Nell, of course.

Granny's Green Punch

1 can of sweetened pineapple juice
1 large bottle of ginger ale
1 quart of lime sherbet

Put the block of lime sherbet in the bottom of a large punch bowl. Pour the cans of juice and ginger ale over the sherbet. You can add these one at a time or simultaneously. Swirl around but do not attempt to break up the ice cream. As the punch is served, the ice cream will melt, causing the punch to take on a creamy consistency.

If you're serving a big group, buy large amounts of juice, ginger ale, and sherbet, and then just keep pouring them into the punch bowl.

For variety, substitute orange, pineapple, or strawberry sherbet for the lime. Vanilla or peach ice cream are also delicious in this drink. If you're using the punch for a wedding, as Lovie often does, you can choose an ice cream to coordinate with the bride's colors. Callie would approve!

Note from Elvis: This recipe has been around a long time, probably in many forms, but the one in this book was handed down from Dorothy Champion, Anita Webb's grandmother. Anita, the author's daughter-in-law, says that when she was a child, she and her cousins thought their grandmother had magical powers because she made their punch turn green. Where have you seen the name "Champion"? Champ, of course—Luke Champion, the vet in the Southern Cousins Mystery series.

Lovie's Prohibition Punch

1 jug of sweet tea (6 cups)
6 c. of sweet lemonade
2 c. of sweet pineapple juice
1½ c. light rum (adjust to taste)
Add some extra dry gin if you're feeling adventurous, but not too much, because the gin will make the punch too tart.

Garnish:
1 sprig of mint
Slices of fresh lemons, limes, and oranges
Fresh strawberries are also good in the summer.

Brew tea the Southern way: steep 6 tea bags for 2 and half minutes in 6 cups of boiling water.

Sweeten to taste while the water is hot so the sugar will melt. Add six cups of sweet lemonade. You can use the commercial kind, but the punch is better if you make the lemonade from scratch with real lemons and all that good pulp. Add 2 cups of sweetened canned pineapple juice.

Add 1½ cups of light rum to taste.

Top with garnishes. Serve in Mason jars over crushed ice.

Note from Elvis: This recipe came from Alice Virginia Daniel, the inspiration for Lovie. She is the author's long-time friend. You can catch Peggy and Alice on the local TV station every Sunday morning sitting side by side in the first soprano section of the choir loft, singing like angels with slightly crooked haloes.

Serve up a batch of Lovie's Southern Fixin's, then sit on the front porch and enjoy reading all of Peggy Webb's Southern Cousins Mysteries.

Elvis has left the building!

Center Point Publishing
600 Brooks Road ● PO Box 1
Thorndike ME 04986-0001 USA

(207) 568-3717

US & Canada:
1 800 929-9108
www.centerpointlargeprint.com